Out of the Dark World

Also by Grace Chetwin
On All Hallows' Eve

Grace Chetwin

Out of the
Dark World

Lothrop, Lee & Shepard Books
New York

*Special acknowledgments to Pam Hoar, Edith Marvell,
and Howard Smallowitz of the Presbyterian Hospital.*

Copyright © 1985 by Grace Chetwin
All rights reserved. No part of this book may be
reproduced or utilized in any form or by any means,
electronic or mechanical, including photocopying,
recording or by any information storage and re-
trieval system, without permission in writing from
the Publisher. Inquiries should be addressed to
Lothrop, Lee & Shepard Books, a division of William
Morrow & Company, Inc., 105 Madison Avenue, New
York, New York 10016.
Printed in the United States of America.
First Edition
1 2 3 4 5 6 7 8 9 10
Library of Congress Cataloging in Publication Data
Chetwin, Grace.
Out of the dark world.
Summary: When a boy whose mind is trapped inside
a computer program begins appearing in her dreams,
eighth-grader Meg uses a hypnotic trance to summon the
sorceress Morgan le Fay for aid in freeing him.
1. Children's stories, American. [1. Computers—
Fiction. 2. Fantasy] I. Title.
PZ7.C42555Ou 1985 [Fic] 85–5922
ISBN 0–688–04272–4
Book designed by Catherine Stock

For Sallie and Barbara

What seest thou else
In the dark backward and abysm of time?

(William Shakespeare, The Tempest, *I.i.)*

One

Meg walked alone along the empty roadway, her feet making no sound. Smooth gray ridges ran waist-high on either side of her, like banks of dingy ice piled up by giant plows. How had she got onto that road? And where did it lead? She did not know. Beyond the ridges was empty gray, flat as construction paper. No houses, no trees, no telephone poles—not even any sky.

Meg looked ahead. Nothing. Only the gray.

She began to feel uneasy.

The place was lifeless. She must go, out of there. Fast. She turned and hurried her steps back along the road.

When she awoke, she went to the window. The sky was heavy and dark as the gray roofs across the street. It was going to snow.

For a moment her face brightened. Snow on Christmas Eve.

How wonderful.

Then she remembered her nightmare.

It had been years since she'd had one—not since she'd had the mumps, in fact. What had it meant? Every dream told something, Gran Jenkins would say, even if only that you had eaten too much cheese for supper. How she wished for Gran Jenkins at that moment. But Gran Jenkins was back Home in Wales, many miles away. Gran Jenkins had second sight and knew all about dreams and nightmares, and such things. She would talk about them with Meg in a way that Mother never would. Meg also had the Sight, so Gran had told her often since she was very small.

"But how can you know that, when I've never shown a sign of it?"

"You will," Gran had told her, laying a finger along the side of her nose. "You will some day. Just wait and see."

Meg missed Gran very much, even after three years away from her, living in America. They'd been so close. Gran Jenkins would have comforted her and explained what the matter was.

Meg sighed. Mother would have to do. After all, she was also a Jenkins; she also had the Celtic blood. She also had the second sight, some, even if she didn't like talking about it.

She decided to ask Mother about the nightmare during breakfast.

But breakfast was so full of last-minute Christmas shopping plans that Meg never had a moment with Mother alone, and after that she herself forgot all about it.

That night, she and Sue hung their stockings over the mantelpiece, even though, as Meg loudly declared, they were way too old for them now, with Sue in the seventh grade and she herself in eighth. But they'd had the stockings since they'd been born, and anyway, as Meg also declared, for all the large mystery boxes under the tree, they still loved the fun and surprise of finding little things.

"Not at five-thirty in the morning, you won't," Mother warned them, "unless you promise to keep it to yourselves." They promised, and with that she shooed them off to bed so she could wrap the last of the gifts.

It was not until Meg was dropping off to sleep that she remembered her nightmare. Oh well, maybe tomorrow, she thought. And again—maybe not.

For tomorrow was Christmas Day.

— — —

Meg stood on the roadway under the sullen light.

The air was heavy and still.

The ridges seemed closer, longer. Like great gray worms, silent and secret; ice-serpents guarding the sides of the road, penning her in.

She began to walk along the road, slowly, and without thinking at first, then faster. All at once, she became aware of a queer pulling sensation in her head. She was being drawn forward along that road, against her will.

She tried to stop. To resist. Danger lay that way. She could feel the cold of it curling out toward her. She struggled, fighting to slow her feet but still they kept moving, faster, until the very road seemed to roll under her, moving her on into, what? Terrified now, she called out.

"No! Mother! Sue!"

A hand gripped her shoulder.

". . . Meg? Shh! Guess what! It's snowing! It's snowing! And look!"

Meg opened her eyes a slit to find her bedside light on and Sue crouched beside her, dangling their bulging stockings in her hands. The hand holding Meg's stocking was pressed against Meg's shoulder.

"Meg?"

Sue let Meg's stocking go on top of her.

Meg closed her eyes in relief, cuddling her lumpy stocking. Good old Sue for waking her. The nightmare—her *second* nightmare—was losing its hold. The road, ice-serpents, were giving place to familiar things.

Yet the sense of danger lingered.

Sue shook out her stocking happily onto Meg's comforter.

"Hey, Meg! Look!" Sue spread her things around, then held them up one by one. "I got saltwater taffy, and notepaper, and . . . *six* markers and ribbons and . . . two pairs of leg warmers and a book of cryptograms and—look at this neat little shoulder bag!"

Meg laid aside her stocking and, climbing out of bed, pulled aside her window shade. White flakes flocked the dark glass, slid down to pile onto the sill.

Meg let the shade fall, glanced back at her clock.

Four-forty-five.

Definitely too early to wake Mother. Maybe she could tell Sue about it. She looked over to Sue flipping through the pages of her new puzzle book and decided not. She hated fuss, and Sue loved a drama. No, strong as the dream was upon her, she would still wait to tell Mother about it first.

Going back to her bed, she took her stocking and dumped its contents out.

And Christmas Day began.

— — —

Not once during the whole day did Meg have Mother alone.

That night Mother and Father went to a late, late party.

That was when Meg smuggled the old clown nightlight out of the bathroom cabinet and hid it under her pillow, ready to plug it in the moment she was left alone.

Mother came in smelling of new perfume. She sat on the edge of the bed and kissed the tip of Meg's nose.

"If you need anything, our number's by the phone." Her face went worried. "You've been so quiet, Meg. What's wrong?"

Meg sat up on one elbow. Now was the time. Now at last she could tell Mother about the dream.

But Father had other ideas. He and Mother were late, he called from the bottom of the stairs. If they were any later they'd arrive just as everyone else was going home.

Mother stood up. "Meg?"

"I'm fine, Mother," Meg lied. "Except for too much turkey."

Mother laughed. "I'll buy that! Okay, I'll look in on you when I get back. It was a good day, wasn't it?"

Meg smiled and nodded. Meg nodded Mother out and down the stairs. A good day. As good a Christmas as ever they'd had. It was the thought of the night that bothered her.

— — —

Meg decided to read for a while. She crossed to her bookshelf, picked out a favorite book, a collection of ancient Welsh bardic tales called *The Mabinogion*. She turned the pages until she came to the story she liked best: the tale of Prince Pwyll of Dyfed and his bride, Rhiannon, who some said was also Morgan le Fay, King Arthur's witch sister. Meg just reached the best bit where Pwyll first saw Morgan le Fay in her "garment of shining gold brocaded silk," riding toward him on a "big fine pale white horse," when she saw that it was time for lights out.

She finished the page, plugged in the nightlight, then flipped the main wall switch and slid down under her covers.

She closed her eyes, then opened them again. She couldn't bear the thought of going off to sleep again alone. Maybe she'd go and tell Sue about the dream after all. Sue's room was next door.

"Sue?"

She touched Sue's shoulder. "Sue? Sue, wake up!"

Nothing.

Sue went down every night like a tropical sun. And there was about as much chance of bringing one back as the other.

Meg sighed and crept back to bed. Maybe it was just as well. But now she was determined not to risk that scary road again. She'd stay awake until Mother got home by counting sheep. It was bound to work, because she'd never gotten to sleep doing that yet!

— — —

The air over the road seemed thick with quiet. On either side the ice-serpents had reared their glassy backs as though in her absence they'd tried frantically to crawl away. Another time Meg would have enjoyed sliding up and down those spiny ridges, but now she wouldn't go near them, not even to get off the road.

How dead it was out there. A road through nothing. Leading where? Nowhere she wanted to go.

Almost at once Meg felt again the queer pulling sensation in her head.

And her feet began to move.

Concentrate, she told herself. Make your feet stand still. But she couldn't. Faster and faster they went until, as before, the road appeared to move under her, speeding her along.

A small black speck appeared on the roadway ahead. She couldn't say why, but the sight of it frightened her.

Was it still, or was it moving to meet her? It was impossible to tell. But it was growing larger very fast.

It was perfectly round.

Like a dot.

No, not a dot: a small black marble.

Apparently coming straight at her, getting ever bigger and bigger—bigger than a Ping-Pong ball, bigger than a bowling ball, bigger than a basketball, bigger than any ball she'd ever seen. Nearer and nearer it came, a monstrous black snowball about to overtake her.

Turn, turn, she told herself. Go back the other way.

With a great effort, she forced herself around at last and leaned over, pumping her arms, straining to run against the pull in her head and the movement of the road.

Was the ball gaining on her? It must be as big as a house by now, she thought. And looming right over her.

But I won't look, she told herself. I won't.

The ground surely should be shaking, the air filled with its rumbling.

But all was silence.

Out of the silence a voice suddenly cried from right behind her: "Help me!"

Meg looked back—and up.

The gray was gone, the ice-serpents were gone, the light was gone, and the great black thing was rolling over her.

— — —

Meg sat up.

For a moment or two she stared fearfully about the familiar room—at the white shiny dressing table, the oak desk, the music stand sticking up like a praying mantis in the middle of the floor, the bright warm colors on her bookshelves in the glow of the clown nightlight.

Then she jumped out of bed and switched on every light in the place: the ceiling light, the desk light, the lamp on her music stand, the crinolined lady on her dressing table with the light under her parasol, the light on her television set—and the set itself, with the sound off so as not to wake Sue.

There. Now there was light. Plenty of it. The road was gone. And she was safe in bed in Locust Valley, Long Island.

She climbed back into bed and huddled against the pillows with her comforter up to her chin. For the next hour she watched an old grainy movie full of pasty-faced men in baggy pants and wide ties shooting at one another with clumsy guns. Soon Mother would come home and Meg would tell her about the awful nightmare place that was waiting for her somewhere the moment she fell asleep, and somehow Mother would understand and make it go away.

Perhaps.

Two

Meg picked at a cherry tomato at the side of her plate. The fork prongs slid off its slippery skin, sent it skidding under her lettuce.

Lunchtime, and she'd still not managed to corner Mother. No sooner had Father gone off to work leaving Meg and Mother alone than Sue had gotten up, early for once.

Family holidays were all very well, but where was one's privacy?

"It's not fair."

Mother looked up from her book, put her coffee down. "What did you say, Meg?"

"Oh, nothing. What are you doing after lunch?"

Mother looked startled. "Working. Why?"

"I wanted to—"

Sue looked up from *her* book now.

"Oh, nothing." Meg fished for the tomato a second time, sent it rolling across her plate. *Like a marble, a little marble.*

"By the way, Meg." Mother dripped more honey into her coffee and batted it around with her spoon. "Just what were you playing at last night?"

Meg, her face growing hot, glanced across to Sue. Sue looked back to her book, listening all the same. Should she say? No. She still wanted to talk to Mother alone first.

"Well?"

"Nothing," Meg said.

"Nothing?" Mother raised her cup, put it down again. "I come home at two-thirty in the morning to find every lamp in your room fairly blazing away. *And* the television. Even the old nightlight! What's going on, Meg?"

"Nothing. Sorry. I must have dropped off." Meg stared down miserably at her plate, conscious of Sue's curious gaze.

After lunch Mother would go into her study to write. Meg would slip in after her, try to explain.

She thought again about her nightmare.

Three times now she'd had it. Each time there was more and it was worse.

And what about the voice?

Help me!

Was it something to do with her power of second sight? The Sight was a rare gift, Gran Jenkins said, and truth to tell, Meg herself hadn't met anyone else with it outside of Gran's family. And Father didn't have it. Or Sue, who took after him.

"Only those with the Old Blood strong in them have it," Gran said. "Like me and your mother, and you."

Meg had grown up proud of her Celtic blood. Why, even her proper names were Celtic and very old: *Myfanwy,* after Gran Jenkins, and *Gwyneth,* after Gran's elder sister, Great-aunt Gwyneth Jones. She'd taken the name, Meg, only because it was more ordinary and easier for people to say. Meg, made from her initials: *M* for Myfanwy and *G* for Gwyneth.

Night after night when she was small, Meg had listened to Mother's bedtime tales of Druids, of King Arthur, and his witch sister, Morgan le Fay, while Sue had preferred to sit on Father's knee to hear of Paddington, and Christopher Robin, Doctor Dolittle, and Peter Pan.

The idea of the nightmare coming through second sight disturbed Meg even more than the nightmare itself. For the Sight usually warned of trouble and danger, and she didn't want that at all.

Oh, *where* was Gran!

She cornered the tomato at last, and once more raised her fork to strike—unfairly this time, for now she held the slippery thing with her other hand. She struck, and the fork, sliding off the slick tomato skin, jabbed the quick of her thumbnail. She cried out, let go, and the tomato shot across the table, splat onto Sue's open book.

"Meg!"

"Sorry, Sue." Meg took back the tomato, set it on her plate, but the damage was done. A snail's trail of salad oil streaked the page of Sue's brand-new book. Sue had bought it for herself for Christmas, with an early book token. She'd been deep into it since breakfast time.

Meg reached across, took the book, and tried to wipe off the oil, only making matters worse.

"Here," Sue said, reaching for it. "It's all right."

"No, it isn't," said Meg. Nevertheless, she stopped rubbing and squinted at the title. *The Mysteries of Mind Travel* by Dr. Ebenezer Tram. She looked up incredulously. "*Adventures into the Deeper Levels of Consciousness for Fun and Profit?* I thought you were into computers, Sue."

Sue seized the top edge of the book and pulled. "I am. I am."

Meg held on, and book began to seesaw back and forth across the table.

"Girls, girls! You're rocking the coffeepot!"

Meg let go suddenly and Sue shot back in her chair, the book flying back up in her hand.

The doorbell rang. Both she and Sue jumped up and made for the door.

"Hey!" Mother called them back. "Hold your horses! I'll go. You two look too fierce."

Meg subsided, propped her chin on her hands. Now look what she'd done. Spoiled Sue's brand-new book and fought with her into the bargain. What a brat she was being today. Oh, if only she didn't feel so *tired*.

She picked up the little tomato absently with her fingers and popped it into her mouth. For a moment it lay there, cold and tangy with vinegar. Then she bit down and its sharpness exploded on her tongue.

That voice. Who was it calling her? And what did he want?

He?

What had made her say that?

A word came into her head.

Owen.

A word. A name. A Welsh name. First name? Or last? It could be either. It was a good name, a perfectly ordinary name; people called Owen were as common in Wales as minnows in a pond.

Although, for as much time as she'd spent there with Gran and Grandad Jenkins, she didn't know one.

She was so deep in thought that she didn't notice Mother's return, didn't notice her carefully slitting open the cablegram.

Owen. Right out of nowhere the word had popped into her head, and now it wouldn't go away.

"Oh, dear. Dear, dear. That's too bad."

Meg looked up.

Mother dropped the cablegram onto the table.

"It's from Gran Jenkins. Great-aunt Gwyneth died last night."

"Oh," Meg said. How awful, to die on Christmas Day. The thought saddened her but not overly so. Great-aunt Gwyneth was Gran Jenkins's eldest sister, but since she'd lived a fair way from Gran Jenkins, Meg hadn't seen much of her at all. Now Meg was the only Gwyneth left in the family. That thought made her feel lonely somehow.

Great-aunt Gwyneth had been ill for months, ever since Great-uncle Dai Jones's death last year. A mortal blow for her, everyone had said at the time. And so it had been.

"I must—" Mother said, looking around vaguely.

Oh, no. She's going to go into a panic, Meg thought, recognizing the signs. But then Mother suddenly sat down and poured herself the last of the coffee. "I refuse to think of what I must until I've had this."

"You've got to go back Home for the funeral, haven't you?" Sue said. "Can we go, too?"

Mother shook her head distractedly. "Oh, Sue. I'm so sorry. You know we can't afford it. But I shan't be gone long. Maybe a week. Let me see: I'd better call your father first. Then the travel agent. Thank goodness my passport's still valid. Today's Wednesday, isn't it? I hope there's enough money in the account to buy traveler's checks."

Meg was stunned. Mother couldn't leave her; she couldn't! "What about New Year's Eve? And 'Auld Lang Syne'?" *And her nightmare?*

"You'll just have to sing a little louder this year, Meg, that's all. You still have your father, remember? It's lucky that you're off school. But what about your Monday music lesson? How that man can insist on giving violin lessons on New Year's Eve is beyond me. I'll cancel."

She reached for the phone.

"Mother, no!" The idea of canceling the great Professor Koskov shocked Meg, even in this extreme situation. "Father can put me on the train."

Sue reached an arm about Mother's shoulder. "Meg's right, Mother. We'll all manage somehow."

Meg stared at Sue. Manage? What were they saying! By tonight Mother would be *gone!*

Mother drained her cup.

"What a pity," she said. "To think that Great-aunt Gwyneth has died, never knowing to the very end what became of Gareth."

"Gareth? Gareth who?" Meg asked.

Mother looked surprised. "Why, Aunt Gwyneth's son."

"Great-aunt Gwyneth had a son?"

"You didn't know?" Mother sighed. "Well, perhaps you wouldn't. It all happened so long before your time, nobody talks about it anymore. He ran off to sea, and she never saw him again."

"How sad. But why? Why did he run away?"

A buzzing started in Meg's head, and for a moment

everything went dark. Mother's voice came and went in waves that flapped unpleasantly in her inner ear.

When her head cleared, Mother was around the table, bending over her, holding her tight.

"Meg! Meg? Here, drink this." Mother shoved a glass under her nose, a glass reeking of apple cider vinegar, her universal cure.

Meg took the glass, made a face, and drank. As usual, it made her feel sick.

"Have you been having tummy ache?" Mother watched her anxiously.

Meg shook her head.

"My word," Mother said. "I'll have Father remove that television set while I'm gone to make sure you get your proper sleep."

Sue's ears, Meg saw, pricked like a terrier's.

"It isn't that, Mother, honestly. Who," Meg went on quickly, before Mother could speak again, "who do we know by the name of Owen?"

Mother's face went quite strange.

"Owen? Why, Meg? Why do you ask?"

"Oh, I don't know." Had she said something wrong? "My head feels bad. I'm going upstairs."

"Wait, Meg." Mother took Meg's chin and looked her straight in the eye. "Where did you get that name?"

"I—it just came into my head, that's all. Why?"

"Because that was Gareth's last name. Gareth Owen."

Three

Father came home at three-thirty to take Mother to the airport.

The trip was the usual family fiasco, with Mother clutching the car-door handle, yelling for Father to slow down, and Father offering to get out and change seats right then and there in the middle of the icy expressway. Meg found herself doing her bit in the back seat with Sue, over Father's new computer.

" 'Course, it's easy to tell why *you* got into the act," Meg said. "With all those nybbles and bytes and menus and stuff."

"Meg!" Mother kept her eyes fixed front. "That was mean!"

As if Meg didn't know. But her head was aching and she was tired. And she couldn't help being angry with Mother for leaving. Of course, she'd not told her about the nightmares now. How could she? Mother would still have to go and it would only make her worry.

Meg dug again. "Computers aren't that big a deal. I heard on T.V. that the computer brain never will compare with the human mind."

"Whoever said that doesn't know computers," Sue said,

and there they were, off again, until Father shouted for quiet and wished for ejection seats, and Mother shot them one of her grim looks. They went on in silence, Meg wishing that she'd stayed at home.

But it all somehow turned out well in the end, and they finally steered Mother through the departure gate. She looked so tiny in the distance, and so funny all bundled up in her down coat like an unopened Christmas present, backing away around the corner at the far end of the concourse, waving until she disappeared.

Meg squeezed back the tears.

On the way home, Father delivered a pep talk on "doing one's bit and keeping one's chin up." Meg sat untouched by his rhetoric. How did one keep one's chin up when one had sent Mother off right in the middle of the most awful trouble ever? She stared glumly at the back of Sue's head—Sue having beaten Meg to Mother's front seat—then caught Father's eye in the driving mirror to realize it had been on her all the time.

— — —

When they got home, Father lit a fire. Meg helped him, tearing up sheets of newspaper, twisting them, and pushing them under the logs. She loved to help make fires, to watch the flames flare, the sparks fly up the chimney.

Father went out for more logs.

"Keep an eye on it, Meg. Look for sparks spitting onto the rug, and don't let it die down."

Meg nodded. As if she needed telling. She knelt down and tore more paper to feed the flames.

A stray scrap of paper caught her eye, a fragment of a photograph, with bits of print alongside it. It was of a boy in a black sweater with a pirate's face on it and two crossed swords. He'd been doing something with computers, the fragment said, but what Meg couldn't tell, for the rest of the article was missing, even the boy's name.

She searched around for the rest of the page, but it must have already gone into the fire.

She stared at the face. It was familiar. Where had she seen it before? She screwed up the fragment, drew back her hand to throw it into the flames, then stopped, and instead set it by the hearth.

"Meg! What are you doing! The fire's almost out!" Father dropped a load of logs on top of the picture. "Quickly!" He shoved a folded *Newsday* at her. "Fan it! Fan it!"

— — —

As she brushed her hair for bed that evening, Meg suddenly remembered the boy's face.

No wonder it had looked familiar!

She was staring at its twin in her mirror. How odd. They looked so alike, she and the boy. They might be taken for brother and sister! She smiled ruefully. So much for priding herself on looking different. So much for being the Celt!

Her smile faded.

What had she got to smile about? It was bedtime. And nothing was left now between her and the horrible nightmare.

She sat cross-legged on her bed facing the door.

All the lights were on.

Meg picked up a small cloth doll that she'd taken out of her old chest. The doll's name was Big Emmy. Big Emmy had once been Meg's best friend, had once seemed twice Meg's size. How many nights had Meg hidden under her covers from the shadows that came for her over the rows of English chimney pots while Big Emmy sent them packing to pick on someone else?

Meg stroked the threadbare face wishing she could believe in her again. . . .

She held the tattered body to her chest in the old way, rocking to and fro, listening. Father was in his study opposite her bedroom, tinkering with his new computer, alone now that Sue had gone to bed. Meg heard the creak of his chair, the clunk of his coffee mug onto the desk top. She sniffed his bedtime pipe and realized how late it was.

Ten-fifteen. What was Mother doing on the plane? It seemed now that she'd taken off a hundred years ago. To think she wouldn't be landing in England for another three hours at least!

She heard the *thock* of Father knocking the ash from his pipe. Now he'd make his hot cocoa, let in the cats, put out the lights, and go to bed himself.

How empty the house seemed without Mother. And cold. She shivered in her warm, blue pajamas. Meg set Emmy aside and hugged her knees instead.

Father put his head in the door. "Hey, Meg—" he stared around at the brilliance. "What is this? Coney Island? Get these lights out!"

He waited, hand on the doorknob, while she hauled herself over to click off the nightlight, the television, her dressing-table light, her desk light, and her bedside lamp. He waited while she pulled down her bedcovers and climbed into bed, lay down and closed her eyes.

"And don't forget what your mother told you about

watching that idiot box," he added. There was a pause, footsteps, then she was startled to feel a kiss on her cheek. She looked up to find his eyes crinkling down on her. "Goodnight, scamp."

"Goodnight."

The switch beside her door clicked off.

Now there was only the soft glow from the hallway. Then her door closed on that too, leaving her alone in the dark.

She lay curled in a tight ball, listening until his bedroom door finally closed. A moment or two after that, she scrambled around turning everything back on, then laid a sweater against her door to block off the light.

She mustn't fall asleep, she mustn't.

She read some more of *The Mabinogion* until she caught her eyes closing. She crept out to the bathroom, swilled her face with cold water, and carried a cup of it back into her room. Then she began to read once more.

— — —

Meg leaned over, pumping her arms with the effort to run against the backward pull toward the awful black sphere.

But for every step she took forward she seemed to move back two.

She began to tire. She could hear the thump of her heart, and her breath coming loud in the dead quiet.

Behind her, the sphere rolled silently along, its immense bulk swelling.

Now how could she know that?

Turn and look, a voice urged inside her. Quick.

Fearfully, she glanced back, and up, and up . . . and up.

The sphere was not a sphere but a hole, a huge dark hole,

and in front of it was something she'd not noticed from a distance: tiny dancing lights just inside the darkness, a sort of star curtain marking its entrance.

Entrance to what? To black nothing, as far as she could tell. Some horrible Dark World: a void, a trap.

She dug in her heels, sure somehow that once she passed through that star curtain, there'd be no escape.

Even as she struggled, out of the Dark World loomed a face, a young boy's face, a broad Celtic face, like hers; with large sad eyes, pale cheeks, and shaggy black hair. Why, he and Meg might have been brother and sister. On his chest shone a silver pirate's face set against two crossed swords.

"Help! Oh, please help! Is anyone there? I'm locked—"

His face wavered, faded, came again, then was gone.

A lean, sun-browned hand reached out toward her. For a moment it waved blindly about and through the star curtain between them, a drowning hand breaking surface for the last time, then it faded back into the hole.

Meg stared after it, horrified, until she realized she was almost at the star curtain herself.

No! she shouted. Let me go! I won't touch it! I won't!

Four

"*Shh-shush!*" Sue was bending over her, shaking her. "Meg, you were shouting! What's wrong?"

Meg stopped struggling, came awake. She lay rigid, her eyes tight shut against all the brightness, listening for sounds beyond the door. Had she awakened Father, too?

After a moment, she relaxed, looked up at Sue. "Nothing's wrong," she said. The very idea of that place terrified her so much she couldn't bear even to think about it.

"You're sure?" Sue was looking around at all the lights.

"Positive."

"Okay, then." Sue straightened up, turned away.

Meg sat up. "Sue, don't go! Are you thirsty?"

"You bet! Tea or cocoa?"

"Tea."

"I'll make cocoa."

Sighing, Meg turned out all her lights save for the bed-side lamp, and followed Sue downstairs.

The two cats circled the kitchen, purring, then zeroed in on Sue's ankles, demanding a midnight snack.

Meg crept away into the living room and knelt by the hearth.

"What *are* you doing, Meg?" Sue came up to stand behind her.

"Just looking for something. . . ."

One by one, Meg gingerly moved the logs aside, but the newspaper scrap with the boy's face on it was gone. Father must have burned it.

She stood up.

Pity. But no matter. Even without it, Meg was sure it was the same face she'd seen looking out from the Dark World.

Yet though she'd seen him clearly enough, he'd not seen her. *Is anybody there?* he'd called, looking out straight at her. Oh, the sight of his hand disappearing into that awful darkness!

Sue was holding out her mug. Meg took it, led the way back to bed.

Sue, she saw, was carrying not only her own mug but the last of Mother's home-baked oatmeal cookies. Trust Sue. The Great Earth Mother, Meg had called her in an unkind moment. It annoyed her that people took Sue for the older one. But Meg was only too glad of the comfort of her company just then.

Sue perched at the foot of the bed and helped herself to a cookie.

"Now can you tell me what's wrong, Meg?"

"I had a nightmare."

"Oh? What about?"

Meg set down her mug, and pulled her robe tightly about her shoulders.

"I—can't say just now."

"Oh? Mother said today she was getting quite worried

about you, Meg." Sue dabbed the cocoa off her upper lip with her sleeve. "She said you looked terrible. I think so, too."

"She did?" The idea of Mother discussing her with Sue disturbed Meg. She reached for a cookie and began to nibble it slowly around the edges, to make it last.

"Sue, I missed what Mother told us at lunchtime about Gareth Owen. What did she say?"

Sue looked at her curiously. "Not much, with you passing out the way you did. But I asked her more about it while she was packing. She said, let me see . . . that Great-aunt Gwyneth married her first husband—Gareth Owen—when she was only eighteen. Imagine that, Meg. Eighteen. They had a boy named, Gareth. Little Gareth, they called him, so's not to mix him up with his dad. Little Gareth was only fifteen when his father died. And Great-aunt Gwyneth married Great-uncle Dai Jones soon after that.

"Well, Great-uncle Jones and Little Gareth never got on. Things became so bad in the end that the boy ran off. To sea, they said. There were postcards. From Bombay, I think, and from Melbourne and Singapore—and one from New York. Then nothing. Great-aunt Gwyneth never heard from him again." Sue sighed. "How awful, for a child to disappear, and the mother never to know to the end of her days whether it's still alive."

Meg nodded. Yes, terrible. In fact, only the other day she'd seen a mother on the television news whose child had gone off to school and never arrived. The thought frightened her. Imagine Mother if she or Sue disappeared like that!

She swallowed the last of her cookie and picked up her cocoa, staring into it, thinking about the questions piling up on her suddenly. Like the way *Owen* had popped into her mind like that, just when Mother opened the cablegram about Great-aunt Gwyneth. Had Meg perhaps once been told all about Great-aunt Gwyneth and then forgotten about it until the cablegram jogged her memory? That's what Mother had said just before they left for the airport. But Meg knew that Mother hadn't believed it any more than she had.

And then there was the strange boy's face coming at her from the entrance to that awful Dark World—yet, that she could explain by the fact that she'd seen it that evening in the newspaper.

If so, then how did she account for having heard his voice the night before calling out, "Help me"? It *was* the same voice she'd heard, she was sure.

Questions, questions, questions, and no answers. And soon Sue would go back to bed, leaving Meg all alone again to face that awful nightmare.

"Don't you wish," Meg said suddenly, "that you could change bad dreams? Or even better, keep them from coming at all?"

"Oh, but you can, Meg. You can."

Meg felt a rush of hope. "You can?" The hope turned to scorn. "No you can't!"

Sue looked down at the cookie plate. "I'll bet this last cookie that you can."

"You're on." What had Meg to lose? "What do I do?"

Sue slid off the bed. "Wait. I'll fetch Dr. Tram."

"Dr. Tram!" So that was it. "Don't bother," Meg said.

"But it works!"

"How do you know?"

"I just do."

Meg looked at her suspiciously. "Have you tried it?"
Sue always believed what books said, regardless.

"N—no. But trust Dr. Tram."

"To do what?"

"To teach you to go where bad dreams can't get you.
Look, Meg. Just try him. It can do no harm."

"So you say. Oh, all right. Let's have a go."

Sue went to fetch the book.

"Now," she said, opening it at the first chapter. "Here
we go. First he says you lie back and close your eyes.
Then you imagine a wave of relaxation rolling over you—"

"Oh, no I don't." It sounded too much like that awful
hole leading to the Dark World.

"All right," Sue said quickly, flipping through more
pages. "There's another way. Here. On page forty-five.
He says, 'The subject relaxes the body, limb by limb, beginning with the foot.'"

Meg laughed in spite of herself. "What if you have
two?"

"If you're going to be like that . . ."

"Okay, okay. I'm listening."

Sue opened the book again. "When the subject is to-
tally relaxed, begin the countdown."

Countdown?

At the look on Meg's face, Sue snapped the book shut,
stood up.

"Sorry, Sue. Please, I promise, I *promise* I'll be good."

Sue looked angrier than ever. "Oh no you won't.
You're just making fun of me. I thought you were in
trouble. I'm going back to bed."

Sue went to the door.

Meg leaned back against her pillows and closed her eyes. "Okay. Go. But don't blame me for what you might find in the morning."

Sue halted, her hand on the doorknob. "Meg, you ask me to help, then make fun of me and won't even tell me what it's about; it's not fair."

"I know. Sorry, Sue," Meg said. "It's just that it's so scary I can hardly bring myself to talk about it. But, look, I'll try."

Sue went back to sit on the bed while Meg told her right from the beginning. About the nightmares getting worse and worse. About the name *Owen* popping into her head like that. About the boy. And his cry for help. About seeing his face first in the newspaper and then in the entrance to the Dark World.

"Dark World?"

Meg nodded. "As I said, first there was the road, then the dark hole. Then last night I was close enough to see a sort of curtain in front of it, made of lights, like little stars."

"Pretty."

"Oh, no. It's too awful to be pretty. Because through it, inside the hole, there's this Dark World."

"How do you know that, Meg?"

"I just do, you know, the way you always know things in dreams. And I also knew the moment I saw that star curtain that once I went through it, I'd never get out again."

"And that's where you saw the boy."

"Yes. He can't get out, Sue. He tried. I saw him. He

actually got his hand through the curtain. But no more of him. And he couldn't see me, even though I was only a few feet away from him, out on the road."

"How terrible, Meg."

"Yes. And now I'm so scared that tonight I'll go right through that curtain and be trapped just like the boy. What do you think it all means?"

"I think," Sue said in a frightened whisper, "that Great-aunt Gwyneth is trying to give you a message about her son!"

Five

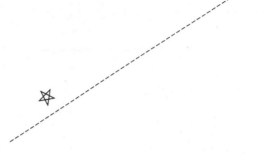

"Her son! Oh, no," Meg said, uncomfortably, conscious that Sue was referring to her second sight. "It can't be that. Sue, the son—Little Gareth Owen—would be older than Mother. Lots older. And it couldn't be a ghost, because the boy I saw was a *today* kid, like us."

"Well, who can he be, then?"

"Beats me. But he's real all right—I mean, there was his picture in the paper. And he's in terrible danger. He's calling and calling for help, and I'm likely the only one who's hearing him. I know I ought to go back and get him out, but I can't, Sue. I'm too scared. Do you blame me?"

"N—no. It's easy to say you should go back, but I'm not so sure I could do it in your place, either. So, what we have to do is keep you off that road—and Dr. Tram can do just that."

"I hope," Meg said. "Okay. Let's get cracking."

Sue reopened the book, and set it on her lap.

"First, close your eyes," said Sue.

Meg closed her eyes, then opened them again and sat up. "It's no use, Sue. I can't. I'm too tensed up."

Sue ran her finger down the page. "He says here, that

if the subject is distraught, he or she must breathe in deeply through the nose and out through the mouth a few times. Try it, Meg."

Meg tried it. And, yes, she began to feel better. Looser. She lay down again and closed her eyes. "Ready, Sue."

"Now," Sue read, in a calm, slow voice, "when you relax the different parts of your body, don't wiggle them or move them at all. Just let them go with your mind. And if you feel a tingling, just breathe out gently through your mouth."

Meg was impressed in spite of herself. Sue certainly was reading the instructions very well.

"Relax your toes," recited Sue. Meg relaxed her toes.

"Relax the ball of the foot. The instep, and the arch."

Which was which, thought Meg, in a brief panic, but she dared not interrupt now.

"Now your heels . . . and ankles . . ."

Step by step Meg let go of her whole body: her legs, her trunk, her shoulders, her arms, her face, her whole head.

In the end, she didn't even feel like raising a finger, and when Sue tested Meg's arm by lifting it, it flopped back onto the bed again as though she were dead to the world.

Sue told her to create for herself a Quiet Place. A place in which to be alone. Meg imagined a garden, a small garden to the rear of Tintagel Castle, King Arthur's birthplace in Cornwall near England's southwest tip. Mother had taken Meg to see the ruins many times, and the tiny bay at the foot of the high cliff where Merlin had waited to pluck the newborn Arthur from the seventh wave of the seventh wave. It was Meg's favorite place.

Morgan le Fay had lived there as a little girl. Maybe if Meg made her Quiet Place there, she might meet the Fay—in her imagination, at least. . . .

Meg made the little garden warm and sunny and sheltered, with a mossy wall, away from prying eyes. She put in it a little stone bench and flowers of all colors, especially roses, old-fashioned roses like the ones on Gran Jenkins's button box.

"Done," Meg murmured, when she was through. She could hardly move her lips.

"Now build three steps leading down into your Quiet Place," Sue whispered. "Three steps wide enough for both feet."

"Done." Meg's voice was barely audible.

"Okay. Now—stand at the top of the steps and look down."

Meg did so and was surprised.

What a beautiful little garden it was.

"Now, Meg," Sue said, close by Meg's ear, "take a deep, deep breath and move down onto the first step with both feet, and say to yourself, *three,* as you let out your breath." Sue stretched the "eeeee."

Meg held her breath, her foot in the air. That boy was still trapped in the Dark World, waiting, hoping. *Is anyone there?* How could she go off and leave him?

"Meg?"

She let out her breath and stepped down.

Threeeeeeeeeeee . . .

She could feel the warm stone on the soles of her feet, cushions of moss in the cracks . . .

When Sue's voice came again it was softer, farther away.

"Now step down again, carefully. Both feet. That's right.

Now take a second, deeper breath, and as you let it out, say to yourself, *twooooo.* . . ."

Two . . . The salt wind smelled of roses.

She faintly heard Sue telling her to take the last step, to count one.

One. Had she said it? Or was she just about to?

The shriek of seagulls overhead drove the question from Meg's mind.

Meg padded across the wiry turf, sat down on the stone bench, and stared out to sea. How blue the sky was, that bright, deep, cold blue you got only in Cornwall. How peaceful.

Her Quiet Place.

She sighed deeply. Looked around at the sleepy flowers nodding in the afternoon heat. Listened to the bees' loud hum. Then she relaxed, closed her eyes, and turned her face up to the sun.

Six

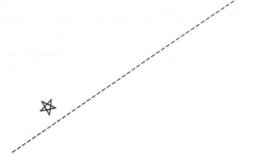

It was nine-thirty when she opened her eyes to bright sunshine.

She jumped out of bed, ran downstairs.

Sue was in the kitchen, watering the grape ivy in the macramé owl hanger over the spice shelves. The two cats were crouched over newly filled bowls, their tail tips waving slowly from side to side.

"Hi, Meg. You okay?"

"Fantastic! I slept like a ton of bricks!"

"I was bringing you a cup of tea, but Father told me to let you sleep."

Meg ran water into the kettle, plugged it in, and sat down at the kitchen table, waiting for the kettle to boil. She not only felt better, she felt like putting in a whole day's practice for her music lesson Monday—which was just as well, it being already Thursday. She hadn't touched her violin all week.

The kettle whistled. Sue took Meg's mug off the shelf, threw in a bag of Morning Thunder tea, filled the mug with boiling water, and set it on the table.

"Thanks, Sue."

"That's okay."

Sue made them slices of toast and plastered them thickly with peanut butter. Then she sat down opposite Meg. "Can I go into New York with you Monday?"

"In all this slush and snow?"

"Oh, yes. I want to see the lights."

"Okay." Meg bit into her toast. Sue was purposely cashing in on her good mood, Meg knew it. But what did it matter? She owed Sue, quite some.

— — —

Meg set her violin down in disgust.

Nothing was going right. The Bach *Partita* was not the easiest. But she knew how it should sound, and she knew how it was expected to sound by Monday morning, and that was better than this. Where was her circle of concentration that Professor Koskov had taught her to use? "Draw a tight circle all about you, Meg. Like a screen, closing everything out. Now stay in it and ignore everything outside it. And practice!" She'd been doing it for a while now, and it really worked. But not today.

She sat down at her desk, picked up her pen, opened her theory exercise book.

Help! Oh, please help! Is anyone there? I'm locked—
Locked where?

She looked down at the page of her book to find she'd doodled all over it, and in ink.

Five-pointed stars.

Pentacles. Pentangles, as they were called in ancient spell-books. As an amulet it was a sure guard against devils and demons and malevolent warlocks. And it was one of the lucky signs on Gran Jenkins's tarot cards. It always turned up in Meg's tarot readings. It signified wealth. But why, Gran, she'd say. I'm flat broke this week. Ah,

Gran would reply, smiling. Wealth's not just in money, Myfanwy, but in other things too. Yours lies in your music and in your wonderful imagination. Meg would shake her head. If you say so, Gran, she'd say. But I wouldn't mind settling for some extra allowance just right now.

One thing Meg found interesting about the pentacle was that she could draw it without once taking her pen from the paper. Like this:

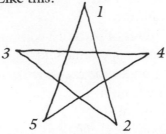

And this was how Meg drew them now, and pretty fast too, though her first attempts long ago had looked more like this:

She stared at the pentacle-covered page and thought again of the boy.

Enough. The day had started so well. Now she was getting morbid again. She decided to look for Sue.

Sue was sitting in Father's study, reading.

Meg leaned against the doorway, sniffing. Leather, polish, tobacco.

"What're you reading, Sue?"

Sue looked up. "This." She slid the open book at Meg across the desk. One of Father's computer books.

Meg took it up. Across both pages were brightly colored photographs of strange, fantastic landscapes. One looked like an aerial view of a housing development with rows of tiny houses, neat streets, and a supermarket here and there. Another picture looked like a weird forest of giant silver cauliflowers.

"They're pictures of parts of a computer taken through an electron microscope," Sue said.

The caption under the cauliflowers read: "Particles of electro-deposited gold for circuit-board connectors," whatever that meant.

"They still look like cauliflowers to me," Meg said. "And I'd say they were made of silver, not gold."

Sue shrugged. "I guess when you view the world at that level, nothing looks how you'd expect it to."

Sliding the book back to Sue, Meg reached out and ran a finger along the plastic cover protecting Father's new computer from dust and cat hair—and idle hands.

"What's this computer like, Sue?"

Sue looked up. "It's different."

"How—different?"

Sue stretched back in Father's chair. "Well, it works even without the keyboard. So anyone can use it."

"Even me?" Meg grinned.

"Oh, yes. Anybody. With the mouse."

"Mouse?"

"This little box. You just point it, press this key on the end of it, and it tells the computer what to do."

"Go on!"

"But it's true."

"Let me see."

"Meg! I can't. Ask Father tonight. He'll show you."

"No. Show me now, and I'll—treat you to lunch Monday."

"Well—I—maybe for just a moment."

Sue took off the cover, set it carefully aside, then slid out a drawer of little floppy disks from a plastic cabinet beside Father's tobacco jar.

"First I have to boot it up."

Sue switched the computer on and slid a disk into a slit in the front.

The screen went a dull gray. Then, after a few quick moves with the mouse, white.

"Oh," Meg said. She'd only ever seen black screens.

"Now," said Sue. "How would you like to—yes! How would you like to write your name on the screen, Meg?"

Meg was impressed. "Oh, why not!"

Sue made a few more moves with the mouse, then, "Watch me," she said. She slid the mouse around on the desk top in front of her. As if by magic, her name crawled in a neat black line across the white screen. "Now you try, Meg. Here."

Sue set Meg's hand over the box, with her finger over the switch, and pointed it at the screen.

Meg moved the mouse. It was not quite as simple as it had looked when Sue did it, but there, underneath Sue's name, as crude as Meg's first pentacles, the word *Myfanwy* appeared.

"Hey!" Meg laughed delightedly. "It works! That's incredible!"

"Okay," Sue said. "Now we'd better—"

"Wait." Meg pushed aside Sue's hand and began to doodle, until the screen fairly rained small black pentacles.

Meg surveyed her handiwork.

"How about printing them out, Sue?"

"No, Meg. It's time to stop."

Meg sat firm. "Oh, come on, Sue, don't be mean. Nothing can happen."

Sue shook her head and reached out to remove the disk.

"Wait! Tell you what. You know that face I saw last night? If I can draw it for you, will you print it out?"

"Oh, Meg. Do you think you could?" Sue cleared the screen.

Of course Meg didn't, though when she closed her eyes she could see the boy's face clearly: the high cheekbones and the large, dark eyes. Frightened eyes. And the hair. The thatch of black hair, thick and wiry, like hers . . .

She moved her hand about, willing the lines to form right. What was she doing? She'd gone in there to take her mind off the boy, and there she was drawing him— at least, trying to. It was no use. It didn't look like him at all.

But Sue didn't know that.

"Oh, Meg," she whispered. "Is that him?"

Meg stared at her handiwork. "Yes," she lied. "Now, can we print it out?"

"Okay." Doubtfully, Sue moved around, making the printer hum, tapping a key or two, then suddenly there was a clatter and the paper in the feed began to roll.

"There." Sue tore off the print and handed it to Meg. "Now I'd better get—"

The phone rang.

"It's Mother!" Meg shouted. They ran.

It wasn't Mother at all, but someone hawking magazines. Meg shouted, "We're not in!" and banged down the phone. "Soda, Sue. Give me soda! All this excitement has given me a headache." She sounded so like Mother that she made Sue laugh at last. Sue took two cans from the refrigerator, snapped off the tops, and stuck in straws. Meg sat down, then set the drawing on the kitchen table in front of her.

"It's not so bad. Of course, I'll do much better next time."

"What next time?" Sue said, then stopped, her eyes opening wide.

For suddenly from upstairs came the sound of the printer, clacking away, all by itself.

As one, they ran, scrabbling to be the first up the stairs.

They dashed through the open doorway and stopped dead, looking at the monitor.

Meg's sketch was gone. And in its place was a fully rendered face, a pale face with large dark eyes and a thatch of black hair.

The clacking stopped.

"Oh, Meg. Meg, look!"

Sue lifted the newly printed sheet for her to see.

On it was a perfect likeness of the boy.

Seven

For one instant Meg stood, looking at the sheet, then she moved, fast. Out of Father's study, back across the hall into her own room, where she shut the door and stood with her back against it.

She stared wide-eyed toward her sunny window. As if the horror of the nightmare weren't enough. Now it was coming at her through the safety of broad daylight!

Sue tapped on her door. "Meg? Let me in. It's all right now."

Meg leaned off the door, opened it a crack.

"I've switched the computer off." Sue squeezed through, the two printout sheets in her hand, which she shook at Meg. "Look—what happened just now is perfectly simple. We already had the computer in the MacPaint mode to write our names and draw the picture. And your sketch was still on the screen. You must have nudged the print command by accident when we ran out to answer the phone."

"Oh, yes? Some accident. And how does that explain this?"

She snatched the two sheets from Sue's hand and held them out side by side. "That's some computer, don't you think, changing that for this?" As she spoke she jiggled each sheet in turn; her own amateurish attempt at the boy's likeness, then the perfect printout, like a photograph. "Just look at him, Sue. The eyes. He's scared to *death*. And he's calling for help."

"Meg, you're trembling," Sue said.

Meg didn't answer her but stood staring down at the second printout.

"Hey," said Sue. "Let's make some tea. Mother would. Come on."

Sue tugged at her arm. Meg dropped the sheets onto her bed and followed Sue downstairs.

She sat at the kitchen table and watched Sue take out the little brown pot, drop in two Lipton tea bags, and pour boiling water on them.

"You're still shivering," Sue said.

"Uh-huh." Meg looked down at her arms, still bare from rolling up her shirtsleeves to practice the *Partita,* and found them covered in goosebumps. She rolled down her sleeves and putting her elbows on the table, propped her chin in her hands. How long would all this go on?

And how much worse could it get?

Sue poured the tea, handed Meg a cup.

Meg stared at her tea, thinking of the boy's eyes.

Coward for not going to help him!

She banged her fist down onto the tabletop, making the cups rattle, making Sue jump. "It's no use keeping away, is it? It's coming out after me."

"What is, Meg?"

"The trouble, whatever it is. And it's all to do with that boy."

She took a sip of tea. It was too hot.

Sue said, "What if it was nothing to do with the boy at all? What if somehow your worrying about him caused the computer to print out by itself. Remember that movie about the poltergeist? How it turned out to be the teenager's mind causing the trouble all along and not any ghost or spook or anything?"

Meg stared. She also remembered that teenager being what they'd called "disturbed." Was Sue saying that she was disturbed like that?

"Far out, Sue," she said coldly.

"*Far out*? This whole thing's far out!" Sue sounded hurt.

Meg looked gloomily down at her cup. She'd felt so happy that morning. And now look. But she couldn't blame the boy. Not really. And Sue was right, in a way. At least some of her trouble lay within her head, or rather, her heart.

All morning she'd been trying to forget the boy, and the nightmare. But there he was, all the time; his face looking blindly out at her, his voice calling, "Help me!"

It seemed the only refuge left to her was her Quiet Place, her little garden at Tintagel. But she couldn't stay there for the rest of her life, could she? "So what am I supposed to do now, Sue?"

"Well, perhaps you could—" Sue stopped, looked down at her tea.

"You think I should try going to sleep normally again, don't you? Go back on that awful road."

Sue stared at her unhappily. "It's not for me to say, Meg."

"But that's what you're thinking, all the same. And so am I." Meg pushed back her chair and stood up. "Well, I daren't. I'm not going near that Dark World again for anything. But I'm willing to give Father's computer another go. Come on," she said, and made for the stairs.

— — —

For the next two hours they waited and waited, as if for a telephone call. Meg used almost a whole pad doodling, while Sue read Dr. Tram.

But the screen remained blank, the tiny cursor blinking expectantly.

"Maybe it was just an accident, after all," Sue said. "Or a glitch in the software."

"Glitch?"

"A—a kind of—hitch. You know, a flaw. A malfunction."

"You know it wasn't. He'll come through. Just wait."

The afternoon passed and still nothing happened.

"Meg," Sue sounded anxious. "I'm so sorry. But it's nearly six o'clock. Father will be here any minute. He made me promise not to use it until we'd had a few more sessions together."

"Please, Sue. Give it another five."

The five minutes passed. And another. And another.

"Meg!"

Meg got up wearily. "Well, we tried."

Sue put her arms around her, hugged her tight. "Meg, I'm so sorry. Really I am."

"Thanks," Meg said. "So am I." She went off to her room, not any happier for seeing her violin still lying in its open case, untouched.

Sue was just putting the cover back over the computer when Father's car crunched up the drive.

At that moment, the telephone rang.

This time it really was Mother, faint but clear, and cheerful if tired. Yes, the trip had been fine but slow against terrible crosswinds. And yes, she had driven all the way to Cardiff where Great-aunt Gwyneth was being buried. And yes, Gran Jenkins was already there and definitely in charge, but not too busy to send her love, Mother said.

Meg and Sue spoke to her in turn.

Meg put the phone to her ear. "Meg?" Mother's voice sounded small and very far away, and there was a strange echo. "Meg? Are you all right?"

"Yes, Mother."

"Meg, I've been so worried. Are you still not sleeping?"

Meg could tell by the way Mother asked that she meant much more than that.

"Don't worry," she said. "Listen. Father's here, and Sue. You're not indispensable, young lady."

As Meg had intended, Mother laughed then at hearing her favorite slogan coming back at her like that.

"You little monkey! Meg, seriously, if you should need me, you have Gran's number. I'm only a few hours away, you know."

"I know," Meg said. It was Sue's turn.

Then Father took over.

Yes, they'd all eaten a perfectly good and sensible breakfast. And yes, if Meg felt dizzy again he'd be sure to take her to see Dr. Wylie. For dinner? He'd brought a steaming casserole from the local health food shop, he told her. Meg nodded. That would satisfy Mother. She always said that their casseroles were better than hers, and Meg had to agree. In fact, Father had probably not brought enough.

All too soon the call was over, leaving Meg feeling empty inside, almost wishing Mother hadn't called at all—but not quite.

There was one small consolation.

In Mother's absence, Father called a holiday from the dining table. Instead, he set them all up with trays in the sitting room to watch the news in front of the television.

Meg didn't see any of it. She was thinking of the boy.

"Father," she asked suddenly. "Whose logo is a pirate's face against two crossed swords?"

Father looked at her in surprise. "Why, the Los Angeles Raiders', Meg." He smiled. "You're into football now?"

"Not exactly," Meg said.

The Los Angeles Raiders? Was the boy from Los Angeles? Not necessarily. Meg herself had a Miami Dolphins sweatshirt that Mother had picked up in a sale.

After the news, they played Scrabble.

Father scored fifty bonus points with *miasmal*.

"What," said Sue, "is that!"

Father smiled happily. "You remember those old fogs we called 'pea-soupers' in London? Well, they're miasmal."

"You mean thick and clammy and 'can't-see-a-hand-in-front-of-your-face'?"

"That's right, Sue."

Meg stared into the fire and thought, *Miasmal*: like the gray nothingness over the road leading to the Dark World.

After the game was over she escaped to her room and took out the boy's picture, stared at it for a minute, then stowed it away again.

She doodled some more. Pentacles, all over a brand new pad. Then she practiced—hard—to keep her mind off bedtime and what she now must do.

Eight

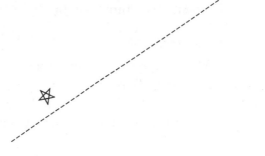

About nine o'clock Father put his head around Meg's door.

"You okay, scamp?"

Meg turned from her music stand, her violin dangling from one hand, her bow from the other. The spot under her chin where the violin rubbed it was red and swollen. Her badge, Professor Koskov called it.

"Yes, thanks. Why?"

"No special reason. I just thought you were going rather hard, that's all." Her father looked at her curiously. "All set for your lesson Monday?"

"I will be."

"Okay. Have fun."

Meg nodded and raised her violin to her shoulder.

Even as the door closed Meg felt the sweat breaking out. She was overdoing the practice, she knew. But it was either practice or go crazy.

One more hour to bedtime.

She began to play.

— — —

When Sue crept in with Dr. Tram's book, Meg was waiting.

"I shan't need him tonight, Sue. I'm not going to my Quiet Place after all."

"What!"

"What happened this afternoon won't necessarily ever happen again. You were right. I'm going to have to go to sleep normally. Have that nightmare."

"But you can't, Meg. I won't let you! You might never come back!"

"You can't stop me. I'll fall asleep sometime."

"Meg, there might be another way to reach the Dark World safely—or *more* safely, anyhow. I was just reading about it this afternoon."

"How?"

"You go to your Deep Place and work from there."

"What do you mean, 'Deep Place'?"

"It's like this: you go to your Quiet Place then down some more."

"How much more?"

"Another twenty steps."

Sue sat down cross-legged on the floor, opened out the Tram book well past the halfway point.

"What's the idea of going to this Deep Place, Sue?"

"Well, this way you're still in charge. You build a lab for yourself down there. Equip it with anything you like depending on what you need."

"Like what, Sue?"

"Well, maybe you can use it as an observation room with a plate glass wall. You know, like in Captain Nemo's submarine in *Twenty Thousand Leagues Under the Sea*. That way you can look out on the Dark World without getting sucked in."

Meg looked doubtful. "I don't know. All I'll probably

see through the plate glass wall is the gray road. It's pretty long. And anyway, even if I can stand in my lab looking out at the Dark World, what's the use of that? It won't help the boy."

"True. But Dr. Tram says wonderful things can happen in one's lab. So there's no harm in going down there just to see what other ideas you might get."

"Will you go with me?"

Sue shook her head. "I can't. I can't get into your mind, can I? Well? Would you like to try?"

Meg certainly would. It sounded a whole lot better than just lying down and waiting for the worst to happen. "What do I do?"

Meg was to build her lab however she wanted it, Sue said.

"But there're a couple of things Dr. Tram says you have to have in it, Meg. One's a command chair—a bit like our hairdresser's chair, I'd say. With a control button on each arm."

"What for?"

"I haven't read that bit yet, Meg. I'll go through it while you make your lab. Now the other thing you must make is a closet door that slides not sideways, but *downward,* into the floor. And make it closed."

"How weird. Whatever for? I know, I know. You haven't read it yet. Okay, here goes."

Meg closed her eyes and pictured the lab, a large rectangular place, like the gym at school, with daylight panels in the ceiling and shiny white floors and walls—except for the far end wall which, using Sue's idea, she made of plate glass.

She made the command chair red and set it on a pedestal. It was soft and comfortable, with a high back and wide arms with a large control button on each one, ready to hand. It did look rather grand, Meg thought, looking all around it with satisfaction. Like a throne. She decided to curve the arms a bit, color the two control buttons bright blue, and the pedestal gold.

She set the closet door next to the entrance, facing the plate glass wall. She made it high and wide but without a handle. What was the use of a handle on a door that opened from the ceiling down?

She described her handiwork to Sue. "What do I do now?"

"You make twenty steps to take you down to your lab, through the floor of your Quiet Place, any which way you like."

Meg decided on a flight of spiral stone steps winding down from a hole in the grass beside her garden seat. At the bottom of the steps she made a passage leading to a wooden door. A lovely, thick, solid door, with a big brass knob: the entrance to her lab.

"Done," Meg said. "Now what?"

"There's just one more thing," Sue said, running her finger quickly down the page. "There'll be two people waiting down there for you, Meg."

"*People?*" Meg frowned. "What people? I didn't plan people."

"I'm afraid you have no choice. They're your guides. Dr. Tram says that when you build your lab, you automatically get two guides, one male, and one female, 'born of your innermost psyche—' "

"Whatever does that mean, Sue?"

"I don't know. But that's what he says here."

"Can I pick them?"

"No. You have to take who comes. Oh, I envy you, Meg. It'll be like opening two giant Christmas presents."

"Presents? You mean they'll be wrapped up in the middle of the floor?"

"Nnn—no. They come through the closet door, one at a time. As soon as you get down there, you sit in your command chair and with those two control buttons, you open that door twice. The left-hand button slides the door down, the right-hand button closes it up again. The man comes out first, then the woman. Got it?"

Meg nodded. "Got it."

"Dr. Tram says, 'Don't be nervous when they come toward you. They are there only to protect and guide you.' Now, here's how you greet them—and don't mess up because they're not your servants and if you offend them in any way, they might refuse to help you. First, you ask their names. Second, where they're from. Third, what they do. Then you ask them to come and stand by you, the man on your right, the woman on your left. And these are the exact words you must use. . . ."

Meg listened, growing restless. Do this, do that. Say this, say that. What a fuss. Guides! Maybe she could ignore them. She'd much rather go it alone. Unless . . . Her heart quickened.

But no. Hadn't Sue said that you couldn't pick them? She sighed as she lay down at last. Because she couldn't help thinking as Sue began to read her down to her Quiet Place how splendid it would be for Morgan le Fay to appear.

Nine

Her little garden looked so peaceful and inviting that she lingered for a moment feeling the warmth of the sun.

Through a small round hole in the grass beside her stone seat, the twenty new steps wound down to her lab.

She stood quite still for a moment, poised above them, listening to the lap of waves down in the bay. Suddenly, she didn't want to leave. Didn't want to go to her lab. To face those two strange people waiting for her. To go back to the Dark World, and trouble.

Her mind wavered, the opening in the grass went fuzzy around the edges. She shook herself. You're going, my girl, like it or no. Now—*form your circle of concentration!*

She started down cautiously, feeling her way along the wall. It was cold and damp and studded with little cushions of moss.

The steps were rough, uneven, and the murky daylight reached no farther than the third one. She looked upward with longing to the small circle of blue sky, then with a sigh, she set wrought iron sconces down the spiral wall, bearing torches. Then she continued around and down by the torches' ragged light; twelve, thirteen, fourteen . . .

How dank it smelled down there. Musty.

. . . nineteen . . . twenty.

With relief she stepped onto the passage floor.

It was very dim down there. The light from the sconces in the stairwell flickered in the draft. They couldn't have seen very well at night in the days of King Arthur, thought Meg. Electricity was so much better.

At once before her, at the end of the passage, a small red neon sign appeared above the door.

"Entrance to Lab," it read.

She took hold of the large doorknob, turned it, and pushed.

With a loud creak it opened, and she was inside.

There was her lab, exactly as she'd made it!

It was big and bare as her school gymnasium, and even smelled a bit like it. It was light and clean, just as she'd pictured it, with floor and walls of shiny white, and the red command chair in the middle.

Facing her was the plate glass wall, as planned. But to her surprise, it was quite dark. Strange. She'd expected to see either the gray road, or the star curtain in front of the black hole.

She moved across the floor and pressed her nose up against the glass but all she could see was a reflection of herself and the lighted room behind her. She smacked the glass in disgust. Fat lot of use it was going to be if she couldn't see through it! It occurred to her then that she might be actually *inside* the Dark World!

She firmly pushed that thought aside and made for her command chair.

Climbing into it, she swiveled it around to face the two

doors: the door she'd come in by and the closet door beside it.

She fingered the bright blue control buttons in the arms. One in the left arm, the other in the right. Now to summon her two guides.

First the man.

Meg pressed the blue button at her left hand.

At first, nothing seemed to be happening, then she realized that very, very slowly the closet door had begun to descend.

Her hands tightened on the arms of her chair. Who? she wondered. Who was waiting for her on the other side? Who would she like it to be? King Arthur? Now that she came down to it, she thought not. He was good, but maybe too good. He never could see when someone was cheating him right under his nose. Sir Lancelot? Sir Galahad? No. He'd make her feel uncomfortable, being so perfect as he was. Sir Kaye, then? Or Sir Bedivere?

Her face grew warm with excitement.

She watched the darkness widening as the door came down inch by inch. Saw the top of a head. A grizzled head of thick hair atop a sun-browned brow, then the bluest, keenest eyes she'd ever seen, staring straight out at her, unblinking as a mariner's scouring the horizon for land. Then a high hooked nose. Then the mouth. When you're trying to guess what someone is like, Gran Jenkins always said, look for the mouth, not the eyes. Eyes can lie, but not the mouth. Meg stared at the man's mouth. It didn't look grim, or mean, yet it didn't look entirely kindly, either.

Now the whole face showed over the top of the descending door, a weathered face, clean-shaven. All angles and planes like wet clay under the thumb.

Below the face was a red scarf, a kerchief knotted by the ear.

And still the door inched down.

His shoulders were not too broad, but they were straight. The body was lean, dressed in a rough blue tunic with the sleeves rolled up to the elbows. Below the tunic were stout brown leggings laced to the knees and great hard boots of the sort that Welsh miners wore.

Well. She'd certainly not seen *him* before. And he certainly wasn't anything to do with King Arthur. She wasn't at all sure she was going to like him.

"What is your name?" she asked him, just as Sue had told her to.

The man stepped from the closet with a heavy tread but came no nearer. "My name? Why, 'tis Peter Saltifer, by all the stars," he said.

The voice was clear, a little harsh, with rolling *r*s.

"Where are you from, Peter Saltifer?"

"I come from Nowhere and Everywhere. I fly no flag. I carry no bag. I wear no badge. I am a Man of the World."

Meg stared across to him. What a strange thing to say. Even tramps carried some possessions around with them. And yet, come to think of it, a free soul like that might have free ideas. Which was just what she needed.

"What do you do, Peter Saltifer?"

"I speak truth. That is what I do. And let none gainsay it."

Meg leaned back. Great. A lot of use he was going to be, after all. She didn't want truth. She wanted inspiration. It was a good thing Sue had told her exactly what words to use, or she might say something she shouldn't.

"Thank you for coming, Peter," she said. "If you would step over here to my right hand, I'll now greet my woman guide."

Don't be nervous when they come toward you. Meg remembered Sue's words. *They're there only to protect you and guide you . . .*

Even so, as he clumped over, Meg swallowed, trying not to look as scared as she felt—until, as he reached her, she caught a faint tang of sweet earth from the cloth of his tunic that reminded her of Gran Jenkins's back garden with its rows of beans and lettuce and potatoes and raspberry canes.

She decided to like him after all.

She pressed the button on her right, closing up the door again.

"It's so good of you to have come," Meg said warmly.

Peter turned his head to look at her. "That it's not. I'm here because I'm here. Because you pushed that button. I had no say in it."

Meg, stiffening, leaned away from him. Well! To think she'd decided to like him! If that was how he felt, he could just go back where he came from and she'd pick somebody else.

"I can't. And you can't," Peter said. "Because I'm what you got whether we like it or not. I come from the deepest part of you. I *am* you, in a way."

Meg didn't like the sound of that. She would have argued the point but she'd already pressed the "down" button again.

The door began to move. Who was waiting on the other side? She wouldn't even think her name. Oh, she couldn't bear the suspense. The door was not down an inch before Meg covered her eyes and turned her head away.

She counted to ten. Fifteen. Twenty. Was it open yet? She dared not look. Instead, she parted her fingers a slit, watched Peter watching the door.

Peter suddenly grunted and straightened up, hastily crossing himself. "You'd better look now," he said. "She's full to view."

Meg lowered her hands.

"Good gracious!" she cried softly and got to her feet.

Ten

At first Meg could not believe her eyes.

In that cramped, shadowy space stood a horse, and on the horse sat a woman.

For a moment, neither the horse nor the woman moved. Then, just as Meg was beginning to wonder if she'd not gotten a life-sized statue for a female guide, the woman jiggled the reins.

There was a sharp *clack-clock* of iron shoes, a soft snuffle, and into the light rode the woman on a high white horse with black hooves and a long white mane.

Meg's eyes shone, and for a moment she quite forgot to breathe.

It *was* Rhiannon-Morgan le Fay, it had to be! On her "big fine pale white horse!" She was even wearing the same "garment of shining gold brocaded silk" mentioned in *The Mabinogion*.

The Fay's features never were described in the book, but Meg was glad to see that her hair was as black and bushy as Meg's own, and her eyes just as dark.

By all that was wonderful! Meg couldn't believe her luck.

Meg opened her mouth to greet her as she was supposed to do, but Morgan le Fay, ignoring her completely, rode around the floor in a wide arc, fetching up beside Peter.

"Well, Merlin! It's been long!"

Peter spun around to face her. "You know full well I'm no Merlin. My name is Peter Saltifer, by all the stars and let none gainsay it! Get you away from me, you lamia!"

Meg caught her breath. *Lamia!* The serpent-witch that lured young men to their deaths! She closed her eyes, fearing an explosion.

But the Fay only laughed. A light, clear laugh that made Meg want to laugh too, although she knew she shouldn't. "Aha! You're right! You couldn't be that one, for you're too strait!" She reached down to touch him.

"Back!" Peter cried, raising his arm so suddenly that Morgan le Fay's horse reared and retreated several paces on its hind legs.

Morgan le Fay steadied the horse, brought it about beside Peter again.

"Dog!" she cried. "Take care how you speak to me! Lamia, indeed!" She smiled suddenly and lowered her voice. "Shape-changer I may be, but never the snake!"

Peter turned his keen blue eyes on her.

"You warned me of my rudeness. What about your own, woman? This maid here waits to greet you."

The Fay looked past Peter to Meg still standing in front of her command chair and for the first time their eyes truly met.

Oh, please, Meg thought, feeling the blood flush her face. Please don't be mean to me. I couldn't bear it.

"You—girl—by what magic art did you summon me? Well? What say you?"

Say? Meg swallowed and fell back on Sue's drill. "What is your name?"

"Which one would you like?" Again the Fay's laugh, the irrepressible laugh that tugged at the corners of Meg's mouth. "Ah, the maid has a sense of humor. Call me Morgan le Fay, the name you most know me by."

"Where are you from, Morgan le Fay?"

The Fay turned and pointed to the closet door. "Out of there, and an uncomfortable moment I had of it until your magic released me."

Magic? Did the Fay think *her* a witch?

"And what do you do?"

More laughter, shriller this time, which made Meg feel foolish and very, very small.

"Do?" Morgan le Fay tossed back her hair. "I seek truth, of course!"

Peter folded his arms and leaned against the back of the command chair. "You wouldn't know the meaning of that word, woman, if you saw it writ across the firmament!"

"Peter!" The idea of a fight between Peter and the Fay frightened Meg. "Tell me," she said quickly. "I'm now supposed to introduce you to each other. But it looks as if you know each other already. Do you?"

"Aye, in a manner of speaking," Peter said. "As she's the other half of you, you can say we've known *of* each other all your life. But we've never met directly until now."

"You sound as though you don't like her, Peter." Meg felt strangely hurt.

"That I don't. She's too quick and shifty for me. I don't trust her."

"But you must, Peter. You must trust each other. If

you're the two halves of me, don't quarrel, please. I'm going to need you both."

The Fay smiled at her. "Well said, girl. You have sense. What do they call you?"

"Myfanwy, ma'am." Meg bobbed slightly.

"*Myfanwy . . . my fine one* . . . that is a good Welsh name. As for you, my stubborn stone . . ." She nodded to Peter. "For Myfanwy's sake I'll take your apology unspoken." She turned back to Meg. "Tell us what you want of us, girl."

Meg looked, appealing, from one to the other.

"I want to find a boy," she said. "He's in terrible danger."

The Fay's eyes gleamed. "What sort of danger?"

"He's trapped inside a Dark World, and I don't know what it is or how to get him out."

"Oh? Are you sure you should be getting him out?" said the Fay. "Folk who get themselves locked up in those places usually deserve to stay there and everybody is better off for it."

Peter patted Meg's hand. "Tell us about him," he said. "Right from the start."

Meg sat herself back in her command chair and told them of her nightmares, of the black ball that became a dark hole sucking her in. Of the entrance to the Dark World. Of Great-aunt Gwyneth's death. Of Gareth Owen. Of the boy's face looking out from behind the star curtain. Of his hand waving through it, his call for help. Of the computer printout. Of everything that had happened. And as she told it, she thought what a hopeless jumble it must all sound.

Sure enough, when she was done, Peter shook his head.

"Why 'tis such a tangled tale. There is in it not one true line."

"Are you accusing me of lying?" Meg's face grew warm.

"That I'm not," Peter said. "By 'true' I meant 'straight' and 'clear to follow.' That is how truth is, in the end."

"Nonsense." Morgan le Fay slid down from her horse. And Meg saw that although the witch barely reached Peter's shoulder, she stood every bit as straight as he did himself. "Truth is found in many different places. The trick is in finding it and piecing it together. As for the boy, he's obviously under a spell and a common enough one—if powerful. I myself have used it many times." She turned to Meg. "Where is this Dark World that you speak of?"

Meg pointed to the plate glass wall.

"Somewhere out there, I *think*. At least, Sue thinks so."

"Sue?"

Meg curtseyed again, for Sue. "Sue's my sister."

"I see. Is she a witch too? It certainly does run in families." The Fay didn't wait for a reply. "Peter, this is a pretty situation. What say you to it?"

"Nothing—for the time," he said. "I think before *I* speak."

Morgan le Fay reached out and took Meg's hand. The queen's skin was white and soft, her fingers long and finely tapered. Meg was suddenly aware of her own rough calluses and blunt nails.

"Let us seek this boy. Come."

The Fay remounted her horse and gestured Meg up to sit sideways behind her. It took a few tries, but eventually she made it. She looked across to Peter, still standing by her chair. She'd never been on such a high horse. She shifted nervously. To think that women used to ride sidesaddle like this. It didn't feel safe at all.

Morgan le Fay turned the horse and leaned forward, looking down on Peter's mop of hair.

"We leave you to your thinking, Peter Saltifer! May you have joy in it!" she cried. And with that, she nudged the horse forward away from the glass wall and toward the entrance door.

Oh, no, Meg thought. They couldn't go through there. She'd been so excited at getting to sit on the Fay's horse that only now did it occur to her that there was nowhere for it to go.

"You can't—" Meg cried, but even as she did so Morgan le Fay wheeled the horse about and set off toward the dark plate glass wall at a gallop.

"No!" screamed Meg. Morgan le Fay didn't know about plate glass walls. But it was too late.

With a powerful thrust of its haunches, the horse leapt and the next minute, the Fay and Meg were flying forward into the air.

Eleven

Meg shut her eyes and held her breath, waiting for the crash.

There wasn't one.

Only a funny kind of pressure around her ears as though she'd hit water from a high diving board.

Then there came the fast swish of air streaming past.

The Fay's long black hair flapped wildly with the force of it, whipping Meg's face but she daren't let go the Fay's waist to fend it off.

She—holding the Fay's waist!

Under the tight bodice, it was small and hard.

All around them was the gray. And the ice-serpents.

They galloped on. For how long? Ten minutes? Half an hour? Meg had no idea. There was never any sense of real time out on that road. But, she decided, they were taking long enough.

It was indeed a strange journey. There was no sound of hoofbeats, only the rush of air and the horse's breathing.

All at once, Meg felt the telltale pull in her head. Frightened, she peered sideways through the Fay's flowing hair to see the black hole looming ahead with the star curtain shimmering over it.

"Oh!" she cried. "There's the entrance to the Dark World! Slow up!"

"Slow up?" the Fay yelled in her ear. "What sort of witch are you?"

"I'm not one at all!" answered Meg, but the Fay wasn't listening.

Bigger and bigger grew the hole, fast gobbling up the gray. And then it was upon them.

"Stop!" Meg cried and shut her eyes, but the Fay's horse leapt.

— — —

As they passed from light to dark through the star curtain, Meg felt a slight prickling sensation. That was all.

She opened her eyes. All was pitch black around them. Even behind her, where she knew the star curtain and the gray road should be.

She was inside the Dark World.

Meg slackened her hold on the Fay's waist, feeling sick. The Fay moved the horse forward a little way, then pulled up. "Well, girl. We're here." The witch's voice rang loudly through high hollow space.

Metal, Meg thought, in spite of herself. Not stone.

She listened, rigid, waiting for the echoes to die.

"Well? Speak, child!"

The fresh echoes resounded even more loudly than before.

Meg spoke fearfully. How could she tell Morgan le Fay to pipe down?

"I'll call," she whispered, hoping that the Fay would take the hint.

"Hello? Hello?" she called softly.

The Fay's voice came scornfully—and just as loudly—

out of the dark. "You think he hears that?" She laughed. "Tell me now, what has this boy really done and by what magic art did the necromancer shut him in this place? We can't release him until we have the spell, you know."

Spell? What spell? Meg thought frantically. "I—don't know. I only know that he must be here somewhere, because this is the Dark World."

"Then call him again."

Meg called.

As the timid echoes died away, Morgan le Fay startled her by yelling at the top of her lungs.

"Boy? I say, boy! Show yourself!"

Meg held her breath. Nothing, only echoes.

The Fay called again. "Ho there, boy! We've come to fetch you out! There, now. That should bring him." The Fay slid down off her horse.

And who knows who else, Meg thought as she felt the Fay's hands reaching for her to help her down, but she dared not say it.

The floor was smooth and flat and quite solid, but her feet made no sound on it.

She walked forward close beside the Fay. The horse followed behind, its hooves still silent too.

They hadn't gone above a dozen paces when the Fay stopped.

"Hold," she said softly to Meg. "Someone is coming."

Meg held, listening.

The Fay whispered again. "I think we need light." She snapped her fingers and filled the space about them with wild blue fire.

In that instant Meg saw a tunnel of silver wires stretching in tight shining lines away from them to a vanishing point in the darkness beyond. Along that tunnel and toward them ran the boy, in his black and silver Raiders sweatshirt, blue jeans, and dirty white tennis shoes.

All this Meg saw in the brief flare of the Fay's light. Then, like a flash of sheet lightning, it flickered and went out again.

The boy collided with her, gripped her arm. His hand, she remembered, was brown and skinny, though she couldn't see it now. It was also, she now felt, very strong.

"Oh, boy! Am I glad to see someone! Who are you?" He was a good head taller than Meg, as she'd seen in that instant of light.

"Friends. We've come to take you out of here."

"Who's 'we'?"

"Morgan le Fay—and me. I'm Meg, Meg Wilson. Where are we?"

"Standing in the tunnel leading from the main entrance port. How did you get in?"

Port? But there wasn't any water. Oh, well. No time for questions now. "We'll talk later. Let's go," Meg cried, pulling away from him anxiously. They'd been in there long enough.

"I can't! I can't get through the port. I ought to know. I've tried enough times. But you must go while you can. Before he finds you."

"Who?" Meg said. "Before who finds us?"

"The Salleman. Now please—go—before he pulls me back again!"

"Nonsense, boy!" The Fay sounded displeased. "We've come to fetch you and fetch you we will. Here—" Meg heard the Fay's hand patting her horse's side. "Climb up."

She made more brief light to show the way. But the

boy stood his ground. "Will you listen?" His voice came out of the dark. "I *can't* get out! I'm locked in a go to ten in twenty eighty-four."

"You're what?"

"Not now," the Fay said, climbing into the saddle. "I do not like the air in this place. Up, both of you. You first, boy. Here, take hold of my arm."

For a moment, the boy hesitated, then, "What have I got to lose," he said, and climbed up beside the Fay.

"What the—" he said.

"It's a sidesaddle," Meg warned him, too late. She heard him mutter, settle himself in beside the Fay. Then he reached down for her.

Meg grabbed his hand and hauled herself up beside him, half off the saddle now, to the horse's rear.

At that moment, there came a low hum from way down the tunnel, then the distant singing of wires, and Meg felt a faint draft on her face.

"Move! Hurry! Let's go!" the boy shouted. "He's starting the run!"

The Fay wheeled the horse about and urged it back along the tunnel.

In the darkness, Meg gripped the boy tight about the middle, just as she'd done the Fay. *Would they get through the star curtain?* Of course they would. Meg must not let herself doubt it for a minute. They were with the Fay, and she was the most powerful witch in the world. She was immortal. And her real home was the magic land of Avalon.

An instant later, there was a flash, and the boy cried out in pain.

" 'Tis the necromancer!" the Fay called. "He draws his

web over the gate, but he's reckoned without me!" As her horse leapt, she raised her arm and sent out her blue fire but this time it turned back upon her. The Fay cried out sharply as the fire spat and fizzed about her, and Meg, smelling burning, let go of the boy and threw her arms up about her face.

An instant later they were out under the sickly fog. The Fay lay senseless along the horse's neck, her hair flared out around her in a weird black halo.

And the boy had disappeared.

Twelve

"Hey! Where are you!" she screamed back through the star curtain.

No reply.

She realized then that he'd not told her his name.

The horse galloped on, away from the star curtain, fast leaving the Dark World behind.

Meg reached over the Fay for the reins, but in vain. She held onto the Fay instead. Was the horse going right? She hoped so, for there was nothing she could do.

She bit her lip. They'd failed. The boy hadn't made it with them through the star curtain. What had the Fay called it? A web.

And the Fay was lying as if dead, across the horse's neck.

Meg took the Fay's arm and shook it.

"Wake up, wake up!" she cried, but just then the horse suddenly leapt, and they were back in the lab.

The horse came to a stop by the command chair.

Peter was still leaning up against it, his arms folded, looking for all the world as though he hadn't moved since they left.

He caught Meg as she slid down.

"What's wrong with her?"

"I don't know. Oh, Peter, it was awful. We found the Dark World and the boy. He even got up onto the horse between us, but when we hit the star curtain, there was a flash and he—disappeared. The Fay tried to break its power, but her spell turned back on her, and she—she—" Meg could feel the tears starting down her cheeks.

"There, there." Peter put an arm about her awkwardly. "Don't get so upset. We'll have him out."

She clung to him. "Oh, no, Peter. He said—he said no one can get him out. And he was right!"

She remembered the flash of fire curving back onto the Fay, the smell of burning, the Fay's awful cry. *The Fay had failed!*

Meg couldn't believe it.

The Fay was still lying along the horse's neck, face down, her hair all frizzed out like a sticky burr. Was she dead? Could the Fay die after all? The tears started again.

She huddled in the comfort of Peter's arm and wished for Sue. But Sue was up there somewhere, waiting. *I can't get into your mind, can I?* Oh, quit the self-pity, Meg scolded herself and rubbed her eyes.

Peter looked at her with concern. "When I said we'd have him out, it was no lie, maid. We'll do it somehow. You must believe that."

"*Believe* is not enough, Peter. I want to *know!*" Meg cried.

The Fay stirred.

"Don't touch her!" Peter pulled Meg back. "There's bad energy coming off that one. See?"

The Fay stiffened, then convulsed. Her whole body

glowed with a strange green light. Her red lips curled back in a grimace. Her eyes opened suddenly, staring straight at Meg, or through her. Was she in pain? Meg hid her face against Peter's chest, then looked again. The Fay's eyes were shut once more, tight shut as though she'd closed in upon herself. The green light glowed brighter and brighter. Then there came a hissing and Peter held his arms around Meg as sparks from the Fay's hair spattered outward to die in midair.

Suddenly, the green light faded, the Fay went limp again, and her hair fell softly about her face.

Meg held her breath.

The Fay stirred, sighed, and sat up as though from an afternoon nap.

"We're back, I see." She patted her horse's neck. "Where's the boy?"

"He—he—disappeared," Meg said, staying by Peter's side.

The Fay nodded matter-of-factly.

"I expected as much. So the necromancer had his way."

"Is the necromancer stronger than we are?"

The Fay looked down at Meg from her height on the horse. "I wouldn't say that, Myfanwy. But there's magic in that place that's not of rock or tree or hill. A cold magic much different from ours."

"Is it bad magic?"

"It's worse than bad, maid. You see, good magic works a body's good. Bad magic works its ill. But the magic of that place was unmindful of either. It's not natural."

"So, what is there left to do now?"

The Fay's smile was cold.

"Perhaps our man of truth here can . . ."

Meg blinked. The Fay continued to speak but Meg could scarcely hear her.

Peter patted her shoulder. "You've been through a great peril, my wench," he said. "These things take their toll."

Meg nodded dully. Their outlines were beginning to waver in front of her. She was losing control down there. And Sue said that she must not do that while her nightmares lasted. Swaying on her feet now she clasped her hands and faced them both.

"I thank you for your services," she said, only just remembering her drill. "May you rest well. Until I come again, I salute you." She bowed, exhausted, then stumbled toward the door.

Her Quiet Place. She must get to her Quiet Place.

She had a fleeting glimpse of the Fay staring across at her, eyebrows raised, and of Peter standing by her chair. Then she wrenched open the door and ran down the passage.

The door closed behind her as she started up the stairs.

Twenty, nineteen, eighteen, she began. Oh, how tired her body was.

Ten, nine, eight . . . round and round she hauled herself upward, her hands grabbing the rough walls for support.

Three, two, one.

She tumbled up through the opening.

It was dark in the garden. The stars were bright in the high summer sky and the smell of roses was strong.

She must go quickly, three more steps to tell Sue that she was all right. Then back here to her Quiet Place.

She started across the grass . . .

Thirteen

Meg awoke stiff and cold.

Five-thirty-five, her clock-calendar said. Five-thirty-five A.M. on Friday, December the twenty-eighth. The sixth day since her first nightmare.

She rolled over and sat up. The room was ablaze with light. Her bedcovers weren't even turned down. She'd fallen asleep on top of the bed, and there at the foot, lay Sue. Meg touched her hand. It was icy.

She pulled down her comforter and dropped it gently over Sue, then crept out to take a shower.

In the warmth of the steam Meg thought over what had happened, feeling more and more depressed.

She'd been no more successful in going to that Dark World with the Fay than if she'd gone by herself. Except, maybe, that the Fay had gotten them safely out again.

But not the boy. She couldn't get him out, he'd said. And he'd been right.

Well, one thing was for sure. She was never going back. No more lab, no more guides, no more Dark World. What was the point?

What use had the Fay been, for all her talk of magic and necromancers? And Peter Saltifer? He'd done nothing at all. *I think before I speak.* At least the Fay had jumped in to try to help her.

Meg turned off the water. She should talk. She'd done no better. And she'd had hold of the boy. If only she'd held on tighter!

She remembered the flash of fire, the Fay's cry just as they passed through the star curtain. It had to be some kind of force screen across the tunnel entrance keyed to the boy. However many times she went for him, he'd never cross it.

What had the Fay said? *There's a magic in that place that's not of rock or tree or hill. A cold magic much different from ours.*

Magic? Everything was magic to the Fay.

She dried herself vigorously and dressed in warm sweats. When she got back to her room, Sue was waiting with a cup of tea.

"Oh, Meg. What happened? Did you find him? Did you get him out?"

"Yes, I found him. And, no, I couldn't get him out. And I can't, ever. Not even with the Fay."

"The Fay! Oh, Meg, Morgan le Fay was your guide? How exciting."

"I suppose."

"You suppose! What happened? What did she do?"

"We went to the Dark World on her horse. We passed through a sort of star curtain into a tunnel. It's the entrance into the Dark World, the boy said. It was pitch black in there. But when the boy came, the Fay made a kind of lightning flash, and I saw him just for a second. He was exactly how I'd seen him in my nightmares. And how he is on the printout."

Hopeless and scared. But she and the Fay had stirred that hope again. And given him new courage. What had he got to lose, he'd said. And he'd gotten up onto that horse between Meg and the Fay.

His new-found hope had come to nothing. Nothing. Meg had left him worse off than before.

Sue picked up her tea mug, wrapped her hands around it. "So do we try again tonight, Meg?"

"No. There's nothing more I can do. Or the Fay. He told us so."

"What about your male guide?"

"He's no use. If you want to know, he and the Fay argued most of the time. They didn't even like each other! Look, Sue, I've had enough of them, the Dark World, and everything. And I don't want to talk about it anymore. All right?"

"But, Meg," Sue leaned forward, put her arm around Meg's shoulder. "You're just tired, I'll bet. Why don't you go down to your Quiet Place this afternoon. Get some decent sleep, then—"

"*Please*, Sue. Let's leave it."

Sue squeezed her tight. "Okay, if you say so." She slid off the bed, went to the door. "I know I've no right to talk, but remember, Meg: Dr. Tram says your guides are the two halves of you. So when you quit them, you're really quitting yourself!"

— — —

Meg kept to her room all that day, practicing.

At bedtime, Sue came to take her down to her Quiet Place, but Meg sent her away. She could get there by herself now, she said.

And so she did. But when she got there, it wouldn't

go right. She'd wanted to sit in the sun but it persisted in being nighttime. And it was bitterly cold. She sat miserably on the little stone seat, listening to the sea and shivering. Time after time she looked down toward the steps leading to her lab. What were they doing, she wondered, Peter, the Fay, and the boy?

Was the boy watching for her, hoping that she'd go back even after she'd failed? And Peter and the Fay—were they waiting for her, too?

The next day, Saturday, she spent practicing also, going downstairs only by Father's command for tea by the fire and a Scrabble game.

Sue was extra nice to her, not saying anything about the whole thing, which somehow made her feel guiltier than ever.

You mustn't, she told herself. You did all you could. There's nothing left to try.

Sunday afternoon, Father took them out for a walk along the Bayville beach. Meg was looking peaked, he said. She was working too hard.

The wind off the Sound was raw.

"I don't know, Meg," Father said when they got back. "You don't look any better. Don't tell me you're coming down with something. Maybe Mother was right. Maybe you should stay home tomorrow and see Dr. Wylie after all."

"Father! I'll be fine, really I will. I—miss Mother, that's all."

Well, she did. That much was true.

While Father loaded the trays for tea, Meg fed the cats.

She wasn't hungry at all. But she'd have to eat something: Father was watching her. She took her tray to follow Sue and Father into the living room. Four whole hours until bedtime. However was she going to make it?

She sat by the hearth and picked at her food.

Father switched on the news. As usual, they had to sit through the local stuff first.

She didn't want to watch it. She stared into the fire.

But the newscaster's voice broke into her thoughts insistently.

"—enterprising boy, Gavin Thorpe, has allegedly been warned twice before by the F.B.I. for patching into sensitive data banks with his home computer. This daring young man—this talented 'hacker'—was believed to have turned over a new leaf. One week ago he was found lying in a coma in front of his machine."

Meg watched idly as the screen cut from the newsroom to a shot of what was obviously the boy's den: a corner desk crowded with computer, monitor, and a jumble of other electronic equipment, amid the usual clutter of baseball bats, trophies, pennants, empty soda cans, and discarded socks.

The newscaster continued: "Since doctors in California have been unable to diagnose the cause, Gavin was flown into New York this morning and rushed to the Presbyterian Hospital for diagnosis by Dr. Paul Endicott of the Pediatric Neural Unit. Dr. Endicott is the nation's foremost national authority on neural diseases and a Nobel Prize winner. He is also her son's last hope, Gavin's mother, Rose Thorpe said on her arrival with Gavin this morning . . ."

The voice continued over a shot of a loaded stretcher sliding into the open doors of a waiting ambulance.

Moments later, the ambulance sped off down the road,

out of the airport, lights flashing, sirens going full blast.

"Meg!" Sue dug her in the ribs. "Meg, look!"

Meg was looking.

"—and we all join Gavin's parents in wishing him a speedy recovery."

The airport scene had faded to a head-and-shoulders snapshot of the boy, taken with his mother, against a mass of cloudy sky.

It was nothing special: just the usual happy vacation snap found in any family album anywhere in the country. Certainly nothing to interest Meg—except that the last time she'd seen that boy he'd been running toward her along the entrance tunnel to the Dark World!

Fourteen

How she made it through the evening she'd never know, with Father and Sue watching her and not a moment of peace and quiet to think about what she'd seen.

The moment she headed upstairs Sue was at her heels. Not that Meg blamed her. Not after all Sue had done to help.

Meg closed the door behind them, took the printout of the boy's face from her desk drawer and set it on her bed.

Gavin.

"It is him, isn't it?" Sue sounded awed.

"Looks like it."

"What are we going to do, Meg?"

"*I'm* going to bed. You can do whatever you want."

"Oh."

"Sorry, Sue. I'm so tired. Look, I feel as bad as you do. But how many more times do I have to say it? I'd do something if I could. But I can't. So, now let's leave it, okay?"

"But oughtn't we at least to tell somebody about it, Meg?"

Meg spread her hands. "About what? The boy who's

in a coma because he's shut up in a Dark World some-where in my nightmares?" She picked up the boy's pic-ture, put it back in her desk. "Go to bed, Sue. We're off early in the morning, remember?"

"I suppose so. Goodnight." Sue went out.

Meg stared after her. Sue was disappointed with her, she knew. Mother always said Sue had a heart big enough for half a dozen people. Sue wouldn't think twice about going for the boy again. Well, Meg was no Sue, and she wasn't about to start feeling guilty about it.

Briskly, she began to undress for bed.

— — —

Meg sat in her little garden, shivering.

It was always night now, in her Quiet Place. And cold.

But this time, not only was it dark and cold, but it was also raining, a fine misty drizzle that clung to her hair and pajamas. She repeatedly willed herself a raincoat, but in vain.

Gavin.

Gavin Thorpe.

No, not Thorpe. Whatever they said, he was Owen. Gavin Owen. Little Gareth Owen's son. But how? Say Little Gareth had married in the States, then died when Gavin was very small. His widow had obviously taken a new husband, giving Gavin his stepfather's name without ever telling him about his real father. Guesses, guesses, guesses, but she was right; she knew it.

Meg Wilson and Gavin Owen: so alike they might be brother and sister.

Were they cousins? She tried to work it out. Gran Jen-kins and Great-aunt Gwyneth had been sisters. So Mother and Little Gareth had been first cousins. Surely that made Meg and Gavin cousins too.

She brushed the rain off her hair.

Second cousins, maybe.

But they'd not be that for much longer, unless Dr. Paul Endicott could help Gavin.

Gavin's mother had looked so sad and lost at the airport, but still that little bit hopeful—just like that other mother the other day, the one whose son had gone off to school and never arrived.

Meg shuddered.

Dr. Endicott wasn't going to help Gavin, because that other person had him locked up in that Dark World. What had Gavin called him? The Salleman. *Necromancer,* the Fay had called him.

A clever one, to take Gavin's mind and leave his body behind. Oh, what was that awful Dark World, who was that Salleman, and what did he want with Gavin?

She jumped up, suddenly of a mind to go down to her lab. But there were no sconces lit on the stair, and none would light no matter how hard she willed it. Nothing worked right anymore.

It must be her state of mind.

She started down the stair.

Dr. Endicott wasn't Gavin's last hope. She was. Because Gavin was where Dr. Endicott would never reach him. With the Salleman in the Dark World.

She halted three steps down, peering into the darkness, unable to see the bottom. Such cold came up from there. She wrapped her arms about herself and backed up again.

No. She couldn't go down there again no matter what.

Not back to the star curtain. She couldn't help the boy. He'd told her so, hadn't he? She couldn't bear to meet him again. Not ever.

She climbed out onto the grass and went back to her bench, where she sat, looking out to sea.

— — —

The next morning, Father drove them to the station.

"Are you sure you feel well enough, Meg? Are you both wearing enough clothes?" Father swiveled around in his seat.

"Goodness, yes." Meg managed a smile. "If we'd put any more layers on, we'd never have squeezed into the car."

"You're sure your money is safely tucked away?" Father switched off the ignition.

"Sure."

"And you know where to have lunch?"

Meg leaned over and kissed his cheek. "Sure, I'm sure."

Father put one arm around Meg, the other around Sue and gave them both a squeeze. "Keep your wits about you. Remember, even though it's broad daylight, it's still New Year's Eve. There'll be wildness about."

"We will," they both said.

The train clanked in.

Meg snatched up her violin and music case, scrambled out after Sue.

Meg bagged the window seat—an empty victory. The dark green panes were so dirty and old as to be practically opaque. Meg pressed her nose up against the glass to watch the blurry red blob of Father's car turn, ready to pull out of the station lot the moment they were gone.

With a clanking and grinding and a whoop that shook the whole valley, the train moved off.

Meg looked around. Except for the conductor the car was empty.

Sue sat stiffly beside her, the Dr. Tram book unopened on her lap, her face turned the other way.

Meg sighed.

This morning, she'd woken with a headache. And she could think of nothing but the boy.

Sue had hardly spoken a word to her. Admittedly, she'd not left Sue much to say. Meg studied her averted face. She seemed so stiff and unhappy. Maybe if she told Sue *everything* that had happened in the Dark World, they'd both see once and for all that there was really nothing more to be done. And maybe, find some peace. "Sue?" She touched Sue's arm. "I want to talk. About the Dark World."

— — —

By the time they reached Greenvale she'd told Sue in detail of her experiences with Peter and the Fay in the lab. How she and the Fay had leapt through the glass wall. How they'd gone through the star curtain. And met Gavin.

"He came running down the entrance tunnel. It was lined with silver wires. I saw them shining all around him when Morgan le Fay lit it up. He looked so surprised to see us. Almost excited—if only he dared." Meg faltered. "He said, 'Oh, boy! Am I glad to see someone!' "

Meg took out a tissue, blew her nose.

"Oh, Meg. You must be feeling so bad. What did you say?"

Meg looked around.

The train was pulling into Roslyn. A stout lady loaded with shopping bags climbed aboard, halted by their seat, then went on past down to the far end of the car.

"I said I'd come to fetch him out of there. He said he couldn't go. He said the Salleman had locked him in there. He said a lot of funny things, Sue. Things I didn't understand."

"Like what, Meg?"

"He called the star curtain a 'port.'"

"A port?"

"I asked him where we were, you see, and he said, in the tunnel leading from the main entrance port. But that's not all. He said he was locked in a go to ten in twenty eighty-four. Have you any idea what that is, Sue?"

"A go to ten? . . . A *goto 10*?" Sue sat up straight. "That's not a place. A GOTO 10 is a command—a computer command, Meg. You must have misheard."

"No, I didn't and—hush! The conductor's coming."

Meg fished about for her wallet while the big man waited, first on one foot, then the other, clearly of the opinion that she'd had plenty of time to have their fares ready.

"I didn't mishear Sue," Meg insisted when he had gone. "And I couldn't have made it up."

"I suppose not," Sue said, "but it doesn't make sense."

"Why? What is a GOTO 10?"

"It's a loop. Now don't look like that, Meg. It's not so difficult. Say you want the computer to run a five-step program over and over, but you don't want to have to reset it every time. First you list the five steps and give each step a number."

"*Five* steps? What's that got to do with a GOTO *10*?"

"People number the steps in tens, not singles. So step one is called step 10, and step two is called step 20, and so on."

"But why? It doesn't make sense."

"Yes it does. It leaves you room to add extra steps between if you need to after the program is set up. A step 11, say, or 21 or 43. See?"

Meg didn't, but she wouldn't admit it. "So what's a GOTO 10?"

"Remember how I just said that 10 was really 1? Well, after you've set up your last step, called 50, you type 'GOTO 10.' This tells the computer to go back to the beginning. And it does. Every time it reaches 50—or the end—it goes back to 10 and starts over. Again and again, in a continuous loop forever and ever."

"Forever?"

"Or until you pull the plug."

"Oh dear." Meg leaned back and closed her eyes.

"Meg? Meg, are you all right? You've gone ghastly."

Meg nodded, sliding down the seat. Now she knew what the Dark World was and why Gavin couldn't get out.

"He also said, 'Quick! He's starting the run,' Sue."

"Who? Gavin?"

Meg nodded.

"But who, who was starting what run?"

Meg didn't answer her. Her mind was jumping on.

It all fitted.

Check: they'd found him lying in front of his computer at home.

Check: twice before he'd been caught patching into

secret data systems without authorization. A "hacker" they'd called him on television. Twice he'd been caught and twice warned off. Well, obviously Gavin hadn't listened and this time he'd patched into more than he'd bargained for. Someone had not only caught him, someone was keeping him.

Someone? The Salleman.

"He's got to be, Sue," Meg said at last.

"Be what, Meg?"

Meg sat up and put her face close to Sue's.

"Inside a computer."

"Who? Gavin?"

"Who else?"

"In a computer? But that's impossible. And anyway, he's in the hospital. We saw him being taken there last night."

"We saw his *body* being taken there, you mean." Meg leaned forward. "The Dark World is some kind of computer, and Gavin's mind is somehow trapped in it. That's why they can't bring him out of the coma. They can try until they're blue in the face but they won't ever wake him up. I know because he told me. Oh, Sue, he was so scared and alone. And I went off and left him." Meg's eyes went very bright.

Sue took her hand. "No you didn't, Meg. He disappeared."

"It's the same thing," Meg said. Nobody would persuade her differently.

The conductor swung down the car. "Jamaica! Jamaica! Last stop! Please check all your belongings before you leave the train!"

The rest of the passengers gathered their things and stood up.

"I must say though, Meg," Sue said suddenly. "If we're talking about a computer, then *port* does make sense. It's an access point, you see. A way in. But that still doesn't explain the GOTO 10. As I said, GOTO 10 is a command, not a place."

"Exactly. Look, suppose you caught a horse and wanted to keep it from running away. You'd corral it, wouldn't you?"

"I suppose. But what's that got to do with—"

"Please, just listen. Suppose you somehow—just somehow—could trap somebody's mind in a computer. What would you use for a fence?"

Sue looked incredulous. "Oh, come on, Meg!"

"You called it a continuous loop, remember?"

"But how? And who? And why?"

"Which leaves the *twenty eighty-four*."

"Twenty eighty-four?" Sue shook her head. "If that's a command, I haven't heard of it, Meg."

The train slowed, lurched, and clanked forward again.

Meg rocked back and forth on her seat, thinking.

"Gavin said, 'I'm locked in a GOTO 10 in twenty eighty-four' . . . twenty eighty-four . . . *twenty eighty-four!*"

She stood, snatched up her violin and music case.

It wasn't anything to do with computers at all!

"It's time, Sue, don't you see? Gavin's in the Dark World, and the Dark World is a computer. And it's running almost one hundred years from now—in 2084!"

Fifteen

At 11:05 A.M. precisely, the glass door clicked shut behind Meg and Sue as they stood on the top step outside the brownstone building on West Seventy-third Street.

During the last hour, sooty clouds had packed in overhead and random snowflakes were drifting down. Meg set down her violin and music case to zip up her coat, already feeling the mean wind. Hard work and an overheated apartment always left her sweating at the end of her lesson, and she was always so eager to get out and let off steam that she rarely stopped to bundle up.

Her lesson had not gone well. Professor Koskov had griped over and over. "Meg, when will you get the piece together? Last week you play with your head: no mistakes, but cold like scales. This week you play with your heart, but sloppy. Work with both, my dear, and please an old man!"

She'd promised Sue lunch in the coffee shop a few blocks along. Not that Sue should be overly hungry. She'd spent the hour waiting for Meg in Mrs. Koskov's kitchen. The professor's wife was a big, kindly woman, and her cookie jar was always full.

But a promise was a promise.

They ate at first in silence. Meg, at least, was busy with her thoughts. And halfway through the meal she was resolved. She knew exactly where to go and what to do.

"Sue, I've been thinking." Sue looked up from her book. "What we said about Gavin. I—want to go to see him."

"To see him?" Sue closed her book. "You mean—in the hospital? But why?"

"I don't know, exactly. I just do. Will you go along with me?"

"But what good will it do?"

"I don't know that either. Will you?"

"We'll miss the train. Father'll have a fit."

"Will you?"

"Okay."

They paid their check and went out into the snow.

— — —

It was ten stops before they got a seat on the subway. The train was crowded with happy people going home early, already in a festive mood. There was laughing and chatter, and at one end of the car somebody started up a song.

At 120th Street the train emerged into the open air and the darkness of the tunnel gave way to sky.

Meg peered through the dingy glass. She could see no buildings. No rooftops. Only white. And gray. She turned back to the inside. Out there reminded her too much of the road to the Dark World.

It was snowing hard now. Meg felt a touch of nervousness. Sue was right. They really would be home late. But she dared not call Father in case he ordered them back at once because of the snow.

At 125th Street, several people got aboard, spattered

with large flakes that melted at once in the heat of the car.

A black couple wheeled in a baby stroller zipped up in plastic like an oxygen tent. The father steered it down the aisle, the mother bringing up the rear, holding blankets and a nursing bag. As the train jerked forward the father pulled the string of a little music box attached to the stroller handle and at once Meg heard an old familiar tune:

> *Row row row your boat*
> *Gently down the stream*
> *Merrily merrily merrily merrily*
> *Life is but a dream*

Round and round the chimes jingled, in and out of the train's tumult.

Meg found herself thinking, *GOTO 10*. That little round was a sort of GOTO 10 too.

After 129th Street, they were back in the tunnel again. Lights flashed by, dull yellow lights that signaled distant spaces through gaps in the tunnel wall.

Meg jumped at Sue's soft tap.

"Meg? I don't like this."

Meg looked around.

To tell the truth, she didn't either. Everything seemed murkier and more sinister. The stations were covered in so much graffiti that she couldn't even read their names. Only the driver's voice over the intercom told her where they were.

The man sitting opposite was staring at them. At Meg's violin case. He certainly looked tough, with a bony sallow face and stubbly beard. Maybe he thought the violin was valuable. What would she do if he suddenly jumped up and snatched it from her? She remembered an old karate movie on television, saw herself, hands ready, circling the man, then making her move, leaping horizontally through the air toward him yelling "Uggh!" "Ai-eee!" and "Aggh!"

The man stood, swaying and leaning over her. Then, suddenly, he thrust out his fist, making her jump. In it was a sheet of white paper. When she didn't move, he shook it at her and grinned. "Here. It won't bite. Take it."

She glanced at Sue, to find her looking as scared as she felt herself. Nobody else in the car seemed to be taking the slightest bit of notice. The couple with the baby had left the train. Should she scream? She decided against it. Instead, she took the paper just as the train slowed at the next stop.

The man swung out through the open door, onto the platform and away.

As the train moved on and past him, he looked up and waved as if he knew her. The sallow face and waving palm blurred as the train gathered speed.

Who was he?

She had a brief wild idea that maybe the computer man was somehow onto her. That this man was his agent, delivering to her a ticket to . . . where?"

She looked down.

"Fifty cents off at Harry's Diner," the paper said in thick black letters. Somebody had printed underneath in leaky pen, "Judge not lest ye be judged" and "Peace be to all brothers and sisters, amen."

She almost missed their station.

It was much bigger than the ones they'd passed for the

last few stops. The signs read "168th Street" and "Columbia Medical Center."

Meg and Sue stood on the platform while the train moved off with a horrifying sound.

When all was quiet again, Meg looked about them. The other passengers had disappeared over a narrow footbridge spanning the tracks. There was no other way out that Meg could see.

"I'm scared, Meg," Sue said. "It's a long way up here."

"I know," Meg said. "I'm scared too. But we're here now, so we might as well carry on."

They started up over the footbridge.

Meg paused a moment in the middle, staring along the track toward the black mouth of the subway tunnel. Then, "Come on, Sue," she said, and walked on.

Sixteen

Over on the other side of the footbridge, Meg pulled up short. The place was deserted. Where had all those people gone? There were steps but only onto the downtown platform.

Just then, with a faint rumble, doors slid open to their left on the weirdest elevator Meg had ever seen. It was as big as a room and every square inch of its surface was covered in graffiti. It was old and grimy, and the central light sockets were bare.

A woman stood inside, the bulk of her rain cape stark against the busy walls. She looked to Meg like a black enchantress, guarding the secret way out.

"Where's the exit?" Meg asked her—demanded almost.

The woman stepped out. "In there," she said, nodding back into the empty elevator. "Hurry up, honey, or it'll go without you."

In there?

Meg stepped forward cautiously as the doors began to close.

Sue darted in after her.

Clanking and creaking, the elevator began to move.

Meg looked around in the yellow light. How slow it was.

"I don't like it in here, Sue. Do you?" she said. "We don't seem to be getting any place."

"Don't," Sue said. "You're making me scared."

Slowly the doors ground open onto a crowd of people who pushed and shoved their way in as Meg and Sue fought to get out.

To Meg's great relief there were steps ahead, regular steps that led up into the street.

It was as dark as late afternoon, although it was only ten of one and freezing cold.

Luckily the main entrance was just around the corner.

They climbed the steps and went through the revolving doors.

A uniformed guard stopped them.

"Hey! Where you goin'?"

"To see my cousin, Owen, I mean Gavin—"

"Thorpe," Sue said. "Gavin Thorpe."

"You can't go in. Not on your own."

"We're meeting our aunt outside his ward," Meg said quickly. "I forgot the name of it."

The guard consulted a ledger in front of him. "Gavin Thorpe: Pediatrics Intensive Care. South elevator. Ninth floor."

They walked into a central hallway with elevators.

They found the south one, took it. At the ninth floor a woman in a red down coat got out, and they followed her.

Ahead were solid wooden doors, closed. The entrance to the ward?

The woman went to an intercom to the left of the doors and spoke into it, "Mrs. Fleischmann to see Danny."

One door opened, and a nurse came out and beckoned the woman inside.

She was just shutting the door again when she saw Meg and Sue by the elevator.

"Yes?"

Meg found her voice. "I've come to see my cousin."

"Your cousin?" The nurse looked very stern. "Who sent you up here? What's your cousin's name?"

At that moment, the elevator doors opened. In a panic, Meg backed in, Sue after her.

"Hey—" The nurse started toward them.

The doors closed and down they went.

— — —

Back on the ground floor, Meg stood angrily. What a fool she'd been. The nurse had been asking perfectly reasonable questions. But the fact remained that, as the guard had said, children weren't allowed in alone. Officially. And there'd be no *unofficially,* not through those doors.

She sighed. It was all so easy in the movies. There was always a back elevator. Or back stairs. And a handy closet where the heavy put on an orderly's coat and found a handy gurney to wheel around.

Meg decided on the stairs.

"Now, if this is the front of the South wing, Sue, the back must be down here. Come on."

Meg led Sue along the passage leading from the elevator until they reached a door. Stairs.

"Wait here, Sue, will you?" She handed over her violin and music case.

"Meg, what *are* you doing?"

"Going up the back way. I shan't be long."

She ran up before Sue could answer her.

One flight, two, three . . .

What if somebody saw her? she wondered. Once she heard somebody coming up behind her, but they exited onto a floor lower down.

. . . seven flights . . . eight . . . nine.

She halted breathlessly.

According to her reckoning, this was Gavin's back door. She opened it and slipped out.

— — —

Meg found herself in a wide hallway. To her right, a door said, "Pediatrics Intensive Care. Authorized Personnel Only."

She reached the door, opened it a crack. Heard voices, a low laugh. She opened the door a little wider, to see nurses sitting drinking coffee.

Suddenly, Meg heard a commotion. Voices calling, footsteps running. She let go of the door, ran back, then paused.

No one had opened the door. The commotion was nothing to do with her.

It was the intensive care ward, wasn't it? One of the children must be in trouble. Please, *please,* don't let it be Gavin!

She crept back to the door and pushed.

The nurses were moving swiftly away, down to the other end of the ward.

She slipped inside and around the corner, only to dodge back again out of sight. It was an open ward, so open she could see all the way down to the other end, right to the inside of those great front doors she'd seen from the outside. Down the length of the room on either side were cubicles all curtained off.

It was into one of these by the front door that all the nurses had gone.

Meg crept in and was just about to peep through the first curtain when one of the nurses came running out. Meg plunged through the curtain and held her breath. Had she been seen?

The nurse ran past. Meg heard the words, *crash cart*, and there came a faint rumbling as the nurse wheeled something swiftly down to the far end.

Meg stared into the curtain point-blank. What if it were Gavin? What could she do? It might well be. Oh, how could she have left him these past four days to get worse and worse!

Wait, she told herself. That child wasn't Gavin. It mustn't be. He was along there, somewhere, behind one of those curtains, just holding on.

But if so, then how was she going to look for him in this place without being found?

She glanced at the bed behind her and went very still.

No need.

There he was.

— — —

She moved to his side, stunned. Was that the lean brown boy who had run to her in his old sneakers and jeans? Gavin. Her eyes pricked with tears. She'd never dreamed he'd look so bad!

His face was yellow and hollow as an unpainted mask. He looked as empty as the crab shell she'd found once on the beach. Don't cry, Gran Jenkins had told her. He's grown out of it, that's all. In fact, he's probably watching us right now, hiding till his new shell's hard.

Well, Gavin wasn't a crab and this was the only shell he had. And he wasn't here watching either. Because his real self was trapped inside that awful Dark World; exposed, vulnerable as the crab's soft flesh, and dying there too.

She backed off a step. She'd never in all her life before been near dying or death. Had Great-aunt Gwyneth been like this in the end?

She looked around.

Click-hiss . . . click-hiss . . . click-hiss . . .

They called that big green box a respirator. She'd seen one on television. It pumped air in and out of lungs. Meg stared at the air tube up Gavin's nose, at his chest going in and out with the rhythm of the machine, and Meg felt her own breath labor with the pace of it.

She heard now another sound, a high short sound that matched the green wave on the monitor screen: blip—blip—blip—blip—

The beat of Gavin's heart.

There was a second tube up his other nostril and tubes stuck in his arms curving down from drip stands on either side of his bed.

Blip—click-hiss . . .

Oh, Gavin!

She covered her ears.

She remembered him down in the Dark World. He'd been scared, terrified, but he'd been alive.

This boy looked dead. *Was* dead but for those machines.

An empty shell.

She leaned against the edge of the bed, staring at the closed eyes in the sallow face, remembering how dark and wide they had been in her startled glimpse of him. Even in his own trouble he'd been concerned for her without even knowing who she was.

You must go while you can. Before he finds you.

She straightened up angrily. What kind of maniac was this Salleman? She closed her eyes and silently called his name.

Gavin! Gavin!

She felt nothing. No pull. Nothing. And heard nothing but the sounds of the machines. She called again anyway.

Gavin, I'll come for you tonight, I promise!

She opened her eyes. Now she knew why she'd come. To get up the courage to go back into that Dark World to bring him out at last.

But how? Even the Fay could not. If she went back, wouldn't she only end up stuck in there with him? Maybe, yet, she'd go anyway. She and Gavin belonged.

She must go. Quick, before the nurses came.

But yet she couldn't leave him just like that.

She reached forward and touched his arm.

It felt rubbery and . . . cold.

She backed toward the curtain, the feel of his skin still chill on her fingertips. She looked around the cubicle, at the clutter of tubes and bottles and wires, at the tiny white space filled with the cold music of mechanical breath and pulse.

"Tonight," she whispered, and left.

Seventeen

Sue, hovering at the foot of the stairs, looked so relieved to see her. "What took you so long, Meg? What happened?"

Meg looked down. "It was awful. Gavin's buried under a stack of machinery. He looks dead, Sue." The tears started again; she couldn't help it.

"That's terrible," Sue said. "How awful it must have been for you."

"Not as awful as it is for Gavin." Meg scraped her sleeve across her face.

"What we need," said Sue firmly, "is a cup of tea."

"No," Meg said. "We have to get home." She picked up her violin and music case, and started uncertainly down the passage. Which way out?

Sue pulled her back. "No, Meg. Stop a moment. Just a moment. Get your breath back."

Meg let Sue steer her down the hall toward the smell of fried chicken and chocolate cake and into the moist warmth of the cafeteria.

They each chose a slab of the cake and a cup of tea. Sue paid and picked up the tray.

"Meg, you do look awful. Let's find somewhere quiet to sit."

Meg looked around. Her head began to hurt again under the fluorescent light. "I need a window," she said.

They walked the length of the cafeteria, past great pillars painted peachy-orange, past dim murals from bygone days, until they reached daylight at the far end. There they sat looking out on a little snow-covered quadrangle under the dark gray sky. Meg was glad now of the rest. The shock of seeing Gavin had left her shaky.

"I know now why I came, Sue," Meg said at last. "I had to see him, in the real flesh. To get an idea. . . . It was worse, much worse than ever I could have imagined." She fished out a tissue, wiped her eyes.

"And now?"

Even as she said the words, Meg felt the old fear start.

"Tonight, I'm going down to my lab. To bring Gavin out!"

— — —

They arrived home four hours late.

When Meg called Father from the station to pick them up, his voice was tight and strained, but when he arrived he only looked relieved to see them.

"I suppose you went to see the lights," he said, pulling out carefully across the icy road. "Oh, well. I suppose that's what Sue went in for. And I will say that it seems to have agreed with the pair of you. Only next time you're having fun, please let this worrywart know."

Meg and Sue exchanged looks in the back seat. He was letting them off lightly. They should be glad.

"Sorry, Father," they said.

They watched the final minutes of the old year on television, saw the apple fall in Times Square, and drank a toast to the new one, Father with a glass of ale, Meg and Sue with fizzy apple juice.

"To absent friends," Father added, raising his glass again.

"Absent friends," Meg and Sue echoed him. They joined hands and sang "Auld Lang Syne." Meg sang especially loudly for Mother until her voice cracked.

At last they all went off to bed.

Father tucked Meg in.

"Don't feel so bad. I know Mother didn't call, but she did say she might not, because of the funeral."

"I know."

"Four more days and she's home. So cheer up. And Happy New Year."

"Happy New Year—and thanks for not yelling at us."

Father smiled and went out, turning off the lights.

– – –

Meg waited in the dark.

Twelve-thirty. Meg heard Father let in the cats and lock up.

Twelve-forty-five. Father was still in his study. A file drawer opened and shut. What could he be doing? Wouldn't he ever quit? Meg thought of Sue next door and hoped that she was listening too. That she hadn't dropped off to sleep. Although she didn't need Sue to get down to her lab any more, she welcomed the company.

Twelve-fifty.

Sue came in. "I thought Father would never go to bed, didn't you?"

Meg nodded and sat up.

"Are you ready, Meg? Do you still want to go on with it?"

"Yes."

"What are you going to do down there?"

Meg considered. "I don't know yet, but here we go." She lay down and closed her eyes.

Eighteen

The little garden was smothered in warm damp fog. The grass was cold and wet. She stepped cautiously around the bench and down the stairs.

The lab smelled like a stable.

Morgan le Fay was sitting cross-legged at the far end of the room. She didn't move when Meg entered but kept her back turned, staring at the glass wall.

"What's the matter with her?" Meg wriggled up into her command chair beside Peter. "What's this smell? And where's the horse?"

Peter waved his hand over to the closet. "In there," he said. "She sent it in there. It staled all over the floor. The other stuff she threw out there." Peter gestured toward the dark plate glass. "It was mainly hard to clear up, I can tell you. You left us nothing in here. And I for one would have welcomed a modest bite of bread and a mug of ale."

Meg was surprised. It had never occurred to her that they'd be hungry. She set a couple more control buttons in her chair arms and materialized a small buffet set with a mug of Watney's Red Barrel—Father's favorite ale—a plate of cheddar cheese, and one of Mother's home-baked loaves.

"What about the Fay, Peter?"

Peter took a bite of bread and cheese, nodded appreciatively, and swilled it down with ale. "She don't eat. No more she should, one of that kind."

"Peter!" Meg moved toward the closet to look at the horse. How lucky she'd not erased the door!

"You can't," Peter said. "That's only for us. But it's awful cramped in there, I can tell you."

Meg nodded, went back to her seat, and with another button made the closet big as a room—a wide stable filled with oats and sweet hay.

"You're a good girl," Peter said. "Doing all this, with the hurry you're in."

Meg was startled. Hurry! When she hadn't shown up for three days! "Did you talk while I was gone?"

"That we did, my wench."

"And?"

"*She's* decided that you're a figment of her mind, conjured up by Merlin, the wizard. She thinks he's got out of the tree she shut him up in and now he's trying to pay her back. She's 'gone into herself,' as she put it. She says she's going to stay that way until you let her go."

Meg looked over to the Fay. She hadn't moved.

Meg slid down off her chair and ran across to her. "Greetings," she said. "I wish you well and beg your services."

No reply.

Meg squatted beside the Fay. "I'm not from Merlin," she said. "And you're in *my* mind, you know. You're one half of me. And Peter is the other. And you two must come together if I'm to rescue that boy."

Still no answer. No movement at all.

Meg reached out to touch the Fay and recoiled. She didn't feel a barrier exactly, but when her hand reached a certain point she simply lost the desire to move it any closer. She stepped back.

"Look," she said. "This is no good. No wonder I've been having problems up there. How can I get myself together if the two halves of me aren't even on speaking terms? My teacher told me only today—yesterday now, I suppose—how I wasn't getting things together with my music. And you know why? Because you two are like this." She looked to the Fay.

"Sometimes I see things the way you do, ma'am. Then the people up there say I'm 'quick' and 'impulsive' and 'artistic.' Sometimes it works, and sometimes it doesn't, kind of hit and miss."

She turned to Peter. "And sometimes I see with your eyes. Then I'm almost always right, but there's no spark, Peter. So you see until I put the two of you together in my mind, I'll never get anywhere. Not with people, not with my music, or anything that I do.

"So, make friends and accept each other's differences, will you, and let me get on."

Nobody spoke.

"Okay. I'll ask you both again, but not for me. I've got the rest of my life to come to terms with the pair of you, and I mean to, I promise. But right now in the Dark World there's a boy dying, because I can't get him out. And why? Because I'm working with only one half of me at a time.

"Listen, have your differences if you must, but I beg you, just for this night, call a truce. With both of you behind me, I'll be so strong I can't fail."

She went to sit in her command chair. If they didn't come through for Gavin now, she'd never forgive them. Which was to say that she'd never forgive herself.

Peter set down his beer mug and moved around to stand at her right hand. "I've been thinking. What you need, my wench, is a ship. Not one of them great quinquiremes but a trim little craft for tight spots. With a snug wheelhouse to protect you from the elements and glass to let you watch where you're going."

The Fay was on her feet. "Now that, Peter Saltifer, is the first decent thought you've had in your head this night. Let us work on that!" She strode over to her place at Meg's left.

Meg smiled at them both delightedly. "What a wonderful idea. Thank you, Peter. Ma'am."

She shut her eyes waiting for the inspiration to come from the Fay, its practical application from Peter . . .

She needed something nimble that could fly, and fast. Something enclosed to protect her from the road and whatever might lie in store for her, but with a glass cockpit, as Peter had suggested. She'd need a steering wheel, two bucket seats, one behind the other, and lots of controls; booster jets and brakes, a joystick that would let her hover at will, and a panic throttle for emergency stops. The wonderful ideas were coming so fast now that she could scarce keep up with them.

— — —

"Well? What do you think?"

The Fay folded her arms and stared.

Peter walked around it, squinting critically.

It was a sleek silver cylinder: sharp-nosed and blunt-ended with a little glass bubble over the cockpit.

"She don't look like any ship that I've ever sailed on, but she smells trim and lively. Where's the mast?"

Meg surveyed the craft in front of her proudly.

"She won't need one, Peter." She smiled at the Fay. That concept was truly inspired. "She'll run on energy." Meg's own energy. From her own mind.

"No mast? Well, if you say so," he said doubtfully. "All you need now, then, is water to float her, and off you go."

"No water either, Peter. It's a hovercraft."

Meg lifted the glass bubble, climbed in, and lowered it after her.

She selected the largest switch—which looked a little like an auto cigarette lighter—and pulled.

There came from the rear of the car the faintest vibration, then, as Meg pulled out the switch, a quiet hiss and the little car rose from the ground and hovered, bucking slightly, about six inches in the air.

"Well, bosuns and barnacles!" Peter said looking as surprised as can be, but Meg couldn't be sure how much of it was for her benefit. "You forgot your port and starboard lights, though."

Meg pushed a couple of buttons, and at once a red light lit up her right side, a green one her left.

"The *green* ship *left* port if the captain *read right*." Father had taught her that long ago. Peter looked impressed. But Meg didn't stop there. She needed headlights too. What a pity, she thought, feeling the comfortable seat padding grow warm beneath her, that she couldn't take the craft back with her into the upper world.

"Hold!" The Fay walked all around the craft now, her arms upraised, muttering. At once Meg felt such a surge of power go right through her. The ship bucked and danced as though impatient to be off. "Now," the Fay said, "whatever fate falls to the boy, this charmed craft will bear you safely out of that necromancer's lair."

"Oh, thank you, ma'am," Meg said, wishing she could stand up and curtsey.

It was time to go. But before she could move an inch, Peter seized his all but empty ale jug and upended it over the ship's silver nose. A couple of warm flat drops splashed out onto the metal's shiny surface.

"I name thee *Lady Buscarle*!" he cried. "May the winds of fortune speed thee to thy port of call!"

Meg watched the brown dregs trickle down the bright new hull. Well! He might have consulted her first! She'd have supplied champagne for the job. And *Buscarle*! What kind of name was that!

" 'Tis a worthy enough one," Peter told her, eyeing her through the canopy with his keen blue eyes. "It means *mariner* where I come from. 'Tis a name not given lightly, wench."

Meg looked down. "Sorry. And thank you."

"That's all right. Now, slow and steady she goes. Don't go breaking your neck. You'll arrive exactly when you're supposed to however long you take. Good fortune attend thee!"

Peter and the Fay walked the ship to the glass wall.

"Don't be afraid, Myfanwy," the Fay said. "Think only of good things, and you'll get through."

"I will, ma'am, I will. And thank you, both of you." Meg waved a last time, then pulled the lever by her right knee. At once the craft lifted up through the dark wall, past Peter and the Fay and out into the void.

Nineteen

For a moment, Meg panicked. Beneath her, the ice-serpents covered the ground like a maze. There were more roads than she'd ever suspected. And the wind that had whipped the Fay's hair back into Meg's eyes was now a roaring gale. Sheets of gritty dust bombarded the canopy, scratching its smooth surface.

Where should she steer? She made her circle of concentration and kept going straight. In no time at all gray was black, and black was speckled with lights. She was at the star curtain—and through.

The relief was so sudden that her concentration wavered and she nosedived into a stall. Shaking, she sat in the dark of the entrance tunnel. What now? Do what Father does when the car stalls, she told herself.

She waited a minute or two in that awful blackness to let things settle down a bit. She tried to keep her mind free of fearful thoughts—about the Salleman, about how to find Gavin, about whether they would ever get out of there. Instead, she thought about how well she'd done so far and how pleased Gavin would be to see her, just as the Fay had said.   Then she turned on the ignition.

Lady Buscarle started the first time.

Meg switched on the lights and nosed the tiny craft cautiously along the tunnel of bright silver wires, on and on until she came out suddenly into a wide space and had at once the sensation of floating high above the ground.

Now she was *really* inside the Dark World. What was it like? She raised the cockpit cover and leaned out.

The space in which she hovered was dark and vast and ill-defined, with dim oases of light here and there, like the ones she'd seen in the subway tunnel that morning on the way uptown.

It didn't look real at all. But more like a dream place.

Immediately below her was what appeared to be an aerial view of a housing development, with rows of tiny dwellings, neat streets, and a supermarket here and there.

She flew over acres and acres of it, until houses gave way to a curious forest of trees like giant silver cauliflowers that looked strangely familiar.

Why, they were just like the photographs in Father's computer book!

She stared down at the "cauliflower" heads and caught her breath. There, shining in the brilliance of her headlights, she saw a silver pirate's face against two crossed swords.

She flew down closer and there—yes! His shape was unmistakable.

Gavin!

She steered the craft down between two of the strange silvery "trees" and, after parking under one of them, climbed out.

The cauliflower heads that had looked so soft and round from above were hard and unyielding. Metallic.

"They look silver, but they're really gold." His voice

was flat. "According to the data bank they're particles of electro-deposited gold for circuit-board connectors as you'd see them through an electron microscope. And they're antiques."

Antiques? In Father's book they were described as very new. She remembered that here in the Dark World she was in 2084.

Gavin emerged into the light. "The ship's cute. Why did you come back?"

Meg stared at him. He'd changed. In the three days since she'd last seen him he'd grown shadowy, like smoke. The last time he'd looked and felt just as solid as she was.

He also sounded different. As though he actually liked it there.

Had the Salleman been working on him? The thought made her furious.

"To fetch you," she said. "Why else?"

"I already told you." Gavin ran his hand lightly over the scarred surface of Meg's little ship. "I'm locked in. There's no way out, not for me. And not for you, either, if he picks up your mind's energy field. He almost did last time, you know. If that what's-her-name hadn't shorted out the barrier at your exit port, you'd never have made it."

Meg stared. "Gavin Owen," she said. "You sound as though you don't *want* to be rescued. Well, you're going to be, like it or not."

Gavin shook his head. "No I'm not. And my name's *Thorpe,* not *Owen.*"

"Oh no it isn't." She turned her face to him in the full glare of the headlights. "Look at me. See how alike we are? We're cousins."

Gavin shook his head. "I don't get it."

"You will. But now I've got to get you out of here. When you're back up in our own world, you call me, and I'll explain."

Gavin shrugged. "Okay."

Meg told him her number, made him repeat it several times.

This Gavin did, obviously humoring her.

"You're wasting your breath, you know," he told her. "The Salleman will never let me out. And soon it will be too late anyway."

"Nonsense." She raised the canopy. "Get in. We must go. Now."

Gavin looked amused. "You never give up, do you? Well, you would if you knew who you were up against. The Salleman must be the greatest genius who ever lived. Do you know how he found me?"

Meg shook her head, her hand still on the canopy.

"He played me like I was a fish. He sent bait through my home line—data, codes. He had me hooked up half-way around the world. He drew me out, farther, deeper, then—pow! He reeled me in, just like that!" Gavin snapped his fingers. "By *me* I mean my mind, or rather, the pattern of my mind's energy field. He's imprinting it into the computer core."

"But why, Gavin?"

He blew out his cheeks. "You know how back in the 1980s they said that the computer brain couldn't match the human mind?"

Meg nodded shortly. *Back* in the 1980s! She thought of his body *that day* under the tubes and wires. Dying. "Gavin, please, let's go."

Gavin went on conversationally, as though she hadn't spoken. "Well, they still couldn't do any better in the 2080s. Until, along comes this genius with an idea. He says, why don't we combine the computer's brain with a living mind?

"The problem was how to capture the mind's energy pattern and keep it alive. Well, he solved it. He created a biophilic plasma—that's stuff that loves mind energy fields. It prints their patterns perfectly and holds them."

Meg was getting interested in spite of herself. Maybe somewhere in all this, she thought, lay a way of freeing Gavin from this place. "Could it—would it—pick up mine?"

"It could, but right now I'm the only mind programmed to access it."

"What's the plasma like, Gavin?"

He looked pleased at her question. "It looks a bit like gray jelly, which doesn't look like much at all, but I guess you can say it's the mind's life support system."

Life support system!

She remembered the sounds in the hospital cubicle: *Click-hiss . . . click-hiss . . . blip—blip—blip—*

"Anyway, once the mind takes to the plasma, it becomes the core of the computer. The Salleman tried the idea out on a chimp first, a really smart one. Captured its mind's energy pattern, then swung it through the plasma a thousand times via a GOTO 10 just like mine. Time-lapsed just like mine. That means there's a break between each sweep to give the plasma time to absorb the deeper imprint. Isn't that impressive?"

"Gavin, can you stop the GOTO 10 somehow?"

"Oh, no. Once the program's started, not even the

Salleman can stop it until it's completed. It's fail-safe. And why would you want to stop it? Do you realize that when I'm finally imprinted into the plasma I'll live forever? The plasma never deteriorates unless it's exposed to the air, you see."

"So where's the chimp?"

"It didn't work out. The Salleman deleted the program."

"Deleted the program?"

"Cleared the plasma."

Meg was horrified. "Then the chimp died. Gavin, it was hardly immortal!"

"I know. But it couldn't be helped. It just wasn't up to scratch. After that, he went out looking for a computer-compatible human mind. And found mine!"

Meg stared at him horrified. He sounded almost proud. "Why you? Why not pick somebody in 2084?"

"They won't let him."

"Who's 'they'?"

"The Board for Human Sciences. Formed August 2005. When people started using people for all kinds of things—I learned that in here—" Gavin waved his arm around. As if he owned the place, Meg thought. "Well, they checked the Salleman out and decided his idea was—what did they say—'too hazardous for human experiment.' "

Meg stared. How indifferent he sounded. "Gavin, do you remember what they called somebody like the Salleman back in the 1980s?"

He scuffed his toe. "You tell me."

"A murderer. A kidnapper, at least."

"Oh, come on."

She jumped down to stand in front of him. "Listen,

you don't remember, but only three days ago you were desperate to get out. So desperate you reached into my dreams. I came here and saw you trying to get out. That's why I'm here."

"Trying to get *out*?" For a moment, Gavin looked confused. Then he shrugged. "I couldn't have been serious." He leaned against the ship and went on. "After they outlawed him, he fished the back time lanes where they couldn't trace him, to find the sort of mind he wanted. Mine." How smug he sounded. Poor Gavin! She had to get him out of there.

Meg took his arm. Felt with a shock how light it had become, as though it were less there. "Gavin, listen! Do you realize that when your mind's energy pattern is fully imprinted onto that, that—*stuff*—you'll be stuck in there just as the chimp was. Forever—or until he pulls *your* plug."

"He won't. He says I'm A-One First Grade. But even if he does wipe me out, it'll have been worth it. Every time I make a sweep, I learn more and more. Ten more sweeps and I'm done. And I'll know everything every human being has learned from the time of the first squiggles in the mud right up until now. You tell me who else you know who knows everthing in every encyclopedia and dictionary and data bank up to and including the year 2084."

Meg stared at him aghast.

"There! You see? I knew you couldn't." He lifted the cockpit dome and climbed into Meg's seat. "Hop in and I'll show you the plasma—at least, its case."

Meg seized his arm and pulled. "You just get out of

there, Gavin Owen! This ship is mine, and I'll fly it! I don't want to see that horrible stuff. I came to get you out of here!" She was so angry and frightened that she was almost in tears.

Gavin shook his arm free. "Okay. Relax. You drive, and I'll tell you which way to go." He climbed into the rear passenger seat and waited.

Stiff with frustration, Meg scrambled back in and pulled down the canopy.

"We'd better make it quick," Gavin said. "The next sweep's almost due. You must be gone by then or he'll find you. Go straight, that's the shortest way into the center of the dome. Look down there."

Meg looked. Below them was a vast mosaic of tiles glowing under solitary arc-lights like tiny Persian carpets in soft browns and blues.

"Memory chips," Gavin said. "This is still the old part of town. Of course, it's not a town, really, but I like to call it that." Meg glanced back in surprise: his voice had sounded wistful. "Over there." He pointed briskly to the right, "are integrated bubble memory tiles; they were only just coming in back in the 1980s. Now if you want to see the latest—"

Ten more sweeps and I'm done.

Meg pulled up short. "Shut up, shut up, *shut up*! We've got to get out!"

"Now if you're *really* interested, I'll let you see the Salleman. Without his seeing you, of course."

"I don't want—" Meg stopped shouting. Maybe she ought to see him. Father always said that it was better to know your enemy. "How?"

"Easy. Steer over to your left. That's it. Now down."

Meg plunged *Lady Buscarle* through a tangle of cables and wires until they emerged into a vast airy space whose floor was way below out of sight.

"Careful!" Gavin cried. Meg banked right, just missing a narrow catwalk directly below them.

"Where are we?" Meg had a sudden very bad feeling.

"At the central core. Directly below us is the plasma. Look!"

Meg switched on the headlights as Gavin pointed.

She raised the canopy and looked down.

Twenty

Below them, in the glare of the headlights, shone a large silver dome. As big as a large round trampoline, Meg guessed, as far as she could guess anything in that place. The surface of the dome was smooth and unbroken save that at its center was a stopper, like a large gas cap on a car.

Around the edge of the dome, at equal distances apart, stood five short rods. At the tip of each rod shone a cold blue light. From Meg's viewpoint over the dome they looked like lighted candles around a birthday cake. A horrible, hideous birthday cake. The very sight of it frightened her.

"What is that?" she asked, even though she already knew.

"The plasma. Or rather, its casing. The actual plasma's inside. Sealed, the way I said. See that thing right on top of the dome?" Gavin pointed to the "gas cap."

Meg nodded.

"That's the seal. Funny, isn't it, how all this"—Gavin swept his arms about him—"depends on such a little thing."

"What if you took it off?"

Gavin looked shocked. "Don't even think it! Take that

off and the air gets in and—goodbye plasma and good-bye Gavin!"

"What if someone took off the cap before you'd finished imprinting?"

Gavin frowned. "The program would be ruined, I guess."

"And the GOTO 10 broken."

He nodded, his frown deepening. "I guess."

Meg felt a slight twinge of excitement. So there might be a way of stopping this whole thing, after all.

"What are those?" Meg pointed to the five short rods.

"They're the five main access terminals to the entire system. When I make my sweeps I pass through each of those blue lights in turn." He shifted around to look at her. "When I hit those points that stuff floods me so fast I feel ten feet tall."

"Stuff?"

"Data. Input. From everywhere in the system. The world. The universe! When I've hit them all, each time, I imprint."

"How do you do that?"

"I pass through the dome and into the plasma itself."

"And how does that feel?"

Gavin turned away. "Great," he said, but he didn't sound convinced. "Then I take a rest until the Salleman runs me through again."

"Except for your last run, Gavin. You won't be coming out after that."

"That's right." He nodded, then went on, "You see that red and silver tube over to the left?"

Tube? Meg squinted up at the tangle of pipes and wires they'd plunged through. Yes, she saw it, directly overhead, to the left of the catwalk. A thick pipe, big as a water main pipe, snaking down out of the darkness into *Lady Buscarle*'s headlights.

"That's the eye —the computer's eye—*my* eye soon. It can see everywhere, both inside and outside the complex. Come see."

Glad to get away from the dome, Meg lifted the ship alongside the catwalk, then banked left, until they hovered alongside the tube.

"Forward a bit," Gavin said. "You see that bulge in the tube? That's an inspection point. You can look into the pipe from there and see exactly what the computer sees. You want to see the Salleman? Here."

Raising the canopy, Gavin reached out and flipped up a little metal cover in the bulge, revealing a small fish-eye lens. Beside the lens was a tiny switchboard. Gavin flipped a couple of toggles. "There. Now it's set for you to see all the way to the Salleman's control room." He tapped the lens. "Here. Put your eye to that. Go on. It won't bite."

She leaned out, put her eye to the little lens, then started back in alarm.

Gavin laughed. "Don't worry. He's a long way from here. Half a mile away, to be exact. This whole complex is one mile all around, you see, and twenty stories high. But with this eye you can see anywhere you want, just as though you were there."

Meg leaned out and looked again. It was like looking out of a goldfish bowl. There, right in front of her were two men. One man was large with a pink face and white mustache. He was wearing a gray jumpsuit buttoned down the front. The other man was short and square—not much taller than Meg herself—with a short square head, black bushy eyebrows, and a shiny white skull. Gavin didn't have to tell her that this was the Salleman.

He was dressed in plain green overalls, and he was standing with the other man in the center of a big bare room.

"Who's the man in gray?"

"A backer," Gavin said, and Meg heard the pride in his voice. "The Salleman invited him for the last sweeps. As soon as I'm finished imprinting, they'll run a series of tests, and if the backer likes me he'll commission more—on the quiet, of course, until the Board for Human Sciences changes its mind."

Meg eyed the backer in horror. Did that mean more people stolen from the present day? More people suddenly lapsing into comas in front of their computer sets?

Gavin hit another switch, and at once she could hear the Salleman's voice as clearly as if he stood right there in front of them. His voice was low and gutteral. Like mud, Meg thought. And the accent was weird. All clipped and flat, with no *r*s at all. So that's how they'll be talking in a hundred years time, she thought.

"So you see, Mr. Kahn," he was saying, "although there are provisions for human access and maintenance within the complex, it shouldn't be necessary once the final imprint is made."

The man nodded, looking impressed.

"That's because I'll be running everything," Gavin whispered in Meg's ear.

A short buzz sounded somewhere in the room.

"Ah." The Salleman nodded and walked over to the

back wall. "It's time for another sweep. If you'll step this way, you can watch it."

The Salleman pressed a switch and the back wall lit up.

A monitor! Showing the dome, and the space above it, all the way up to the catwalk. Meg pulled back in alarm. Could they see her?

"He's starting the run," Gavin said. "You'd better split." He climbed out of the ship and closed the cockpit.

"No!" Meg cried. "I came for you, and I won't leave without you!"

"Fat chance. Listen. I haven't time to take you out." He pointed across the wide dark space behind them. "Go that way, until you come to the cauliflower forest. From there, follow the old town until you—"

Without warning, Gavin disappeared.

Meg looked around wildly. She wouldn't leave him, she wouldn't. But what was she to do, then?

Before she could decide, there came a faint hum, then the sound of singing wires, just as she'd heard in the entrance tunnel when she'd first met Gavin. Sue! Morgan le Fay! Peter! What do I do? she thought, then the next minute she was caught in a fury of wind and sound.

She formed her circle of concentration, fought to steady the ship, but the wind was too strong for her.

Out, she must get out!

The ship shot forward across the dark space, over the dome, and on toward the cauliflower forest. Even as she saw the silver heads shining in the headlights, she remembered how she'd met Gavin beneath them.

Now she was leaving him again, just when he needed her!

Abruptly, *Lady Buscarle* went into reverse and began speeding back the way she'd come. "No!" she cried, but the ship kept going.

Was that what she really wanted? To go back? *Lady Buscarle* seemed to think so!

When she reached the center again, she pressed a switch marked "Hover," but it didn't work. Instead, *Lady Buscarle* went into another stall.

The ship dropped fast, and straight, right over the plasma dome.

Meg screamed, shut her eyes, and waited for the crash.

Twenty-one

Pull yourself together, she told herself quickly. Remember what the Fay told you. While she was in *Lady Buscarle* she was safe. All she had to do was to think positive thoughts. Like slowing up this fall!

She no sooner thought that than *Lady Buscarle* slowed to float gently downward. But—they were making straight for the dome!

Meg fought to remain calm. Kept saying the Fay's words over and over. Whatever the boy's fate, she'd get out safely in that enchanted craft.

They were almost down when the ship landed on something soft, then bounced off again. For a moment *Lady Buscarle* teetered, then settled.

Meg leaned over and looked out. The ship was lying across the catwalk directly over the plasma dome. She relaxed a little, hoping that the catwalk was strong enough to hold them.

She stared down at the dome with its ghastly blue lights.

Had Gavin started his run?

She'd no sooner thought this than she caught sight of him floating down through the tangled pipes overhead.

For a moment, he hovered, then he began to descend in a long slow spiral around her, narrowing like a funnel, in toward the dome.

Gavin, nearing the end of his run, was preparing to sweep through the plasma!

He reached the terminal nearest the eye-tube first. The moment he touched it, it flared, making Meg blink.

Then he moved counter-clockwise around the edge of the dome to the one on its left. Then the next. And the next. Each about three counts apart. Flash, count one-two-three. Light four. Flash, count one-two-three.

The fifth blue light flared. The circuit was complete!

And Gavin vanished.

The dome began to glow from inside, then flare into brilliance.

Gavin was imprinting!

Meg shut her eyes.

And for one second almost envied Gavin.

Until she remembered asking him how it felt.

Great, he'd said. But his face had told differently.

She opened her eyes.

The light was gone.

The wind was gone.

And the tumult.

Silence.

Calm.

She heard, then, a faint voice in her ear. Dead. Metallic.

"He's picked you up. He's analyzing your energy field. He's trying to decide whether to hold you or delete."

Hold? Delete?

Meg jumped. Gavin was somehow back in his seat, leaning over her!

"Gavin—"

She stopped, appalled. The glow of the instrument panel no longer reflected off his face—it shone right through him!

"Go," he said. "There's nothing for you to stay for. And after you make it home—*if* you make it home—don't ever, and I mean *ever,* come back."

Dully, Meg obeyed him. *Lady Buscarle* began to move, faster and faster across the high space toward the entrance tunnel.

What was she doing? His very voice had mesmerized her.

"Gavin, please . . ." Meg twisted in her seat to plead with him.

But Gavin was gone.

Twenty-two

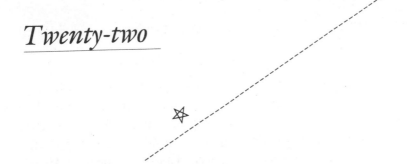

They were waiting for her, watching by the plate glass wall.

Peter helped her climb out onto the lab floor. "Looks like you copped a fair sou'wester out there, wench," he said, and handed her over to the Fay.

"Here, come and sit you down, Myfanwy," the Fay said. She put her arm about Meg and helped her to her command chair.

There, she slumped with her head back and her eyes closed. They were red, she knew, and they must have noticed it, but they didn't say anything.

She began to tell them what had happened, of how Gavin had changed. How she'd tried to persuade him to leave with her, but too late. "He says he doesn't want to come out. But I don't believe him."

"Then go back again. Don't take no for an answer," the Fay said.

"I can't."

"And why not, Myfanwy?"

Meg didn't want to tell them that she was scared, but when she looked into the Fay's eyes, the words came out.

"Gavin says the Salleman will delete me if I go back."

"I see."

"And anyway, it's too late. Gavin's almost finished his runs."

"So what are you going to do, lass?" Peter said.

"I was hoping you'd tell me."

Meg felt the weariness coming over her again. Any minute now everything would go blurry. But it mustn't! Not now! She mustn't give up now!

"There is a way!" she cried. "I just remembered! There's a dome, with a gas cap thing in the middle of it. If only I can get that off before Gavin completes his runs, he'll be free!" She put her hands to her face. "Oh why, why didn't I do it at the time and bring Gavin out with me!"

Peter patted her back. "Because, my lass, you had more sense." He tapped his chest. "I do believe that some part of you had already realized then that you couldn't have done it and let him live. Yes. And 'twas lucky that the Fay did not bring the boy out when she tried."

"Why? Tell us, Peter," Meg cried, even as it began to dawn on her.

"Because he could not have come back *here*! This place is yours, and only yours. There is room for only you in here. That boy would have come to grave harm had he left that place with you. He would have become truly lost. A soul without anchor or harbor."

Or a crab without its shell.

Meg was glad to be sitting down.

The Fay nodded. "Our man of truth speaks well. So what do you suggest, Peter?" she asked him.

Peter stared intently at the floor, then at *Lady Buscarle*'s pitted shell. "Instead of one ship, you need two," he said.

The Fay laughed and clapped her hands in delight.

— — —

It did not take long to make the changes. Meg actually designed them, because neither the Fay nor Peter knew about rocket stages and nose cones. She lengthened *Lady Buscarle*'s body, sharpened the back to match the front, then made each half independent, so that, if all went well, the craft could safely split into two identical halves at the right moment.

Meg turned the back seat to face aft toward a control panel with an automatic pilot and set it for "Gavin's Deep Place," then locked it on "Hold." Then she put in a double-glass partition amidships that she could slide open or shut as she liked.

When she had done, Peter inspected the modified craft for what he called "sea-worthiness," then the Fay walked about it, making extra charms for Gavin's half.

At last Meg was ready to try again. She was just climbing into the cockpit when the Fay took her arm.

"Myfanwy, take this amulet!" The Fay put her hand in a deep pocket of her gown and drew out a very small, very old, silver star-shaped pin studded with tiny stones that flashed with rainbow fire.

"Oh!" Meg's eyes shone. "It's a pentacle!"

The five-pointed star.

"Pentangle," the Fay corrected her. Of course. The Fay would use the ancient word. "This as you would know is a powerful strong sign. And these stones are older even than I. Here." The Fay herself pinned it to Meg's sweatshirt.

Meg fingered the sharp stones. "How very kind of you. Thank you."

Her tiredness forgotten now, she climbed once more into the old front seat—though now front and back looked the same—and bade her two guardians goodbye.

The Fay patted her shoulder. "Good speed. Now, look only forward and follow your heart."

Meg saluted, pulled down the canopy, and flew out into the gray.

She flew high and fast and straight.

With a whoosh she was through the star curtain and into the entrance tunnel. She flew on to the end of the tunnel, out over the little town, the cauliflower forest. There, she faltered, squeezing the pentacle in her anxiety. It was so dark and shadowy. There were no walls or signposts in that vast place. Which way was it to the dome?

Follow your heart . . .

Meg closed her eyes and thought of Gavin.

She moved forward again, until the ship reached a tangle of pipes and wires, which she recognized immediately. She had arrived.

Meg's heart beat faster. Had the Salleman sensed her? Was he even now watching her somehow on one of his monitors? Was he tapping in the order to delete? And would she know it when he did?

Stop it, stop it! she told herself. It's not going to change anything now—except make you mess up. So, where's your circle of concentration?

She tightened her hands on the steering wheel and focused firmly on getting down.

— — —

She parked *Lady Buscarle* alongside the dome and looked out. Her knees were shaking. She couldn't believe she'd actually made it this far. It had been easy enough to talk about from the safety of the lab, but here, now, she wasn't sure she could go through with it after all. She fingered the pin. Look only forward and follow your heart, the Fay had said.

She took a deep breath and stepped out onto the dome.

It looked gray, not silver, in the gloom, Meg having switched off the ship's headlights for safety's sake. Even then she felt so exposed as she moved out from the security of the ship.

The dome was quite flat, now she came to look at it. From where she stood, she could see all the five rods with their lighted blue tips around its base. Access terminals, Gavin had called them.

Before her, in the center of the dome, was the "gas cap."

Was it trying to draw her in?

Not while Gavin was still imprinting.

The fear came again. *If* Gavin was still imprinting.

Steady, she told herself. He was. He had to be.

She reached the gas cap just as the sounds started. She looked up into the gloom, past the catwalk, into the tangle of pipes and wires to where she'd seen Gavin come down the first time.

She stared in dismay. Was that him? That faint dark smudge, right above her?

She seized the gas cap and tugged. It didn't budge an inch.

She tried twisting it, first one way, then the other. But only her hands moved, not the cap.

Around her, the tumult grew, vibrating in her ears,

slapping her hair in her face. Below her, by the edge of the dome, *Lady Buscarle* bucked and bobbed in the growing force of the wind.

Meg hung on, kneeling in the middle of the dome, struggling with the cap.

Until out of the corner of her eye she glimpsed the shadow that Gavin had become alighting by the first terminal.

"Stop!" She stood up, forgetting about the Salleman and his monitor. "Gavin! Stop!"

The shadow touched the rod and the blue light flared.

Round it went, touching each one in turn. Flash, count one-two-three; flash, count one-two-three; flash, count one-two-three; around and around.

Gavin! She couldn't move.

The shadowy figure passed through the dome not two paces from her. The blue light opposite shone right through it. The face, the features were gone. It was just an outline. A faint, shadowy outline of a boy.

The dome lit up under her, dazzling her.

Then the light died.

And the sound.

Was it over? She felt the blood drain from her head. She squatted, put her head between her knees, breathing deeply. Then, as soon as she could move, she went back to the ship.

"Now," she said. "Please, Morgan le Fay, give me inspiration. And Peter, keep it sensible."

She lifted the ship to the catwalk, then flew left to hover alongside the bulge in the eye-tube. She raised the canopy to lean out as Gavin had, hoping that he'd left its setting the same, and squinted through the fish-eye lens.

The Salleman was talking with the backer, waving and pointing to the monitor and shaking his head.

She found the sound switch that Gavin had used and pressed it down.

"But I saw her as plain as plain," the backer said. "Kneeling on the dome as the boy imprinted. Trying to get the seal off, it looked like."

"An illusion, my dear fellow. A slight glitch in the software and easily fixed after this last run."

Slight glitch?

Meg listened, terrified. She remembered Sue, sitting in Father's study, waiting for the boy to contact them again through the computer.

Maybe it was an accident, after all, she'd said. *A glitch in the software.*

That's what the Salleman was claiming she was. A slight glitch.

Easily fixed?

Her first thought was to turn right around and get out of there as fast as *Lady Buscarle* could take her, until she remembered what else the Salleman had said. Gavin was about to make his last run!

Twenty-three

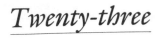

She closed the plate, and looking down toward the dome, noticed a faint shadow hovering over it. Gavin! He'd come out from his imprinting.

She took the ship down.

"Gavin?" If he'd been a shadow before, he was a mere wisp now. She could see right through him—in fact, she could hardly see him at all! She climbed out of the ship, ran to him, to take his arm.

Her hands encountered empty air. There was almost nothing left. He didn't even see or hear her. A moment later, the Gavin shadow disappeared.

The time lapses had certainly shortened.

Any minute now all that racket would start up again and Gavin would start his last run—and so would she if she'd heard the Salleman right!

What could she do?

She thought for a moment, fingering the amulet, then her chin went up.

A glitch, was she? Well, maybe she could prove the Salleman right!

She stared at the dome, and the five terminals, finger-ing the pin. A pentacle. A five-pointed star whose tips formed a circle and which you could draw *without once taking your pen off the paper!*

When Gavin hit the terminals in order, what if she hit them—touched them—out of order? Not in any old sequence. When Gavin made his circle, what if she made a pentacle, which she could make *without leaving the ground?* The lucky pentacle, sure guard against devils and demons and malevolent warlocks! That might break his sequence and jumble everything up.

Glitch in the software, indeed!

She moved to stand ready by the first terminal and mapped out in her mind which terminals she'd have to hit in turn.

By the time she heard the hum, she was ready.

She looked up, saw the faint smudge coming down toward her. Around and around and around, and down.

Another thirty seconds to go . . .

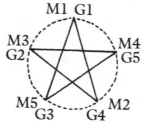

As the shadow hit the first terminal, Meg reached out and seized the rod.

Pain spiked through her, every pain that ever was: smashed thumbs, pinched nerves, drills and needles, and the worst of headaches. She went rigid and her whole body began to shake.

Don't give in, she told herself. You have four more to go!

Flash, count one-two-three.

She wrenched her hand away, feeling instant relief. Gavin moved on to the second terminal.

Meg dashed across the dome to the one on the opposite side.

Reached out and grasped rod four, as Gavin hit the one on the opposite side.

Flash, count one-two-three.

Oh, the pain—oh—oh! She couldn't take it anymore!

Her will faltered. The dome began to waver and lose definition. No!

She tore herself free and moved to her third terminal just as Gavin reached his.

Flash, count one-two-three.

As she touched that third rod, a loud buzzer suddenly sounded overhead. An alarm.

Her plan was working!

Move! Oh, she was tired.

She ran across to her fourth rod hoping that she was still going right.

Flash, count one-two-three.

Thoughts came. Crazy thoughts. Mother slipping on the stairs with an ice-cream cone. Sue trading broken crayons for candy. Father yelling delightedly just once at his old chess machine: Check!

Check!

She reached the last rod. Was she too late?

She looked over to Gavin's last rod just as he reached it.

She'd beaten him by a hair.

Had she beaten the Salleman?

Twenty-four

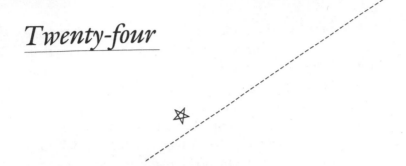

There before her, swaying on his feet, was Gavin; pale, disheveled, but solidly and recognizably himself.

"He's setting up the delete run. For both of us. The GOTO 10's broken and he can't afford to let me loose. . . ."

He sounded exhausted.

He swayed again and almost fell.

Meg caught him. He was going to pass out. She pulled him toward the rear of the ship, braced him against it while she slid his canopy back.

"Climb in," she said. "Gavin, hurry!"

He half fell, half rolled over the side and flopped into his seat, back to back with hers. He slumped forward, his head against his controls.

She strapped him in and stood by her own half, listening to the alarms buzzing back and back through the high open spaces above them.

Should she try to get them out while she could?

What if there weren't enough time?

She glanced to the dome. The terminals were all flashing wildly.

Was it safe anymore? she wondered, and thought, I'll soon find out.

She raced to the middle of the dome. She'd try one more time to take the seal off it. If only she could do that, not only would she and Gavin be safe, but the Salleman would be finished. For good.

She seized the cap and twisted it. No go. She scrabbled at the seal again. Help! Morgan le Fay! Peter!

Anger gave her strength. Anger at what the Salleman had done and still might do. On the very next twist it eased. Not much. But enough.

She rested, then tried again. More. The cap gave a little more. And more. By now her fingers were so tired that as it came up it slipped from her grasp and rolled down into the darkness off the edge of the dome.

Right in front of her was an open hole and through that open hole was the hideous plasma.

She didn't wait to peer down into it. She stood and raced off the dome to the ship. Climbing in, she pulled back the throttle and lifted *Lady Buscarle* up and up and up high above the open hole.

She looked down.

Thick yellow smoke was swishing up from out of it, and she fancied the smell like all the bad smells she could think of: ant nests and clogged drains and Gran's old septic tank; the rat that died in the attic; rotting fish and the hard-boiled egg in her school locker after the Thanksgiving vacation . . .

Smelled good enough to her.

Glitch in the software, indeed!

Had Gavin seen?

He was still lying slumped in his seat.

Pity.

She turned the ship, and headed out.

Twenty-five

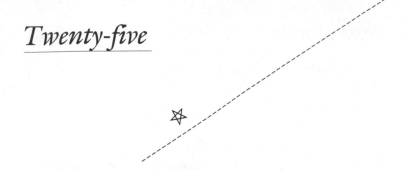

She made it through the star curtain with no trouble and pulled up outside.

Would the Salleman be able to start over with his project?

Hardly.

He'd made a poor showing in front of the backer. He'd not even completed his installation runs. And while Meg might not know much about computers, she did know about backers because Father made presentations to them all the time. Their patience was short, their money was tight, and they didn't like even the *hint* of a hitch—or glitch!

She looked back through the star curtain toward the Dark World.

This was where she'd first seen Gavin.

And now they'd come to the parting of the ways.

She leaned back to check on him.

Dead to the world.

But not dead.

She flipped switches, turned knobs, and activated the automatic pilot marked "Gavin's Deep Place."

As she withdrew to her own cockpit, her fingers acci-

dentally brushed his neck. His skin felt warm and damp.
Alive.

She withdrew her hand, the warmth of him still on her
fingertips. She slid the double-glass partitions shut and
locked them into place.

Okay, Gavin. Here we go.

She pressed a button labeled "Eject."

At once there was a soft explosion somewhere underneath the hull and *Lady Buscarle* split into halves. The
two tiny ships dropped away from each other, each with
a sharp nose and a blunt, glass rear.

She watched Gavin's ship bank sharply up from the
exit port and vanish into the murk. Please, *please* let her
have set his controls right.

She flew low over the ice-serpents, feeling the first
blurriness through her head. Oh, how tired she was now.

— — —

"Here she comes!"

Hands lifted her out of the car.

Her eyelids drooped.

". . . safe now. What about the boy?"

"Gone. His half of the ship with him. She used your
pentangle well."

"Aye, but if he's found safe harbor it's by virtue of your
ship, my fine stone."

Meg smiled at them happily. She'd not only come
through intact, but now she was truly whole. Maybe she'd
master the *Partita* after all!

She wanted to speak, to thank them, to tell them how .
it had all fallen out, but she couldn't. She pointed to the
pentacle pin on her chest, felt the Fay's fingers remov-
ing it.

She felt herself slipping.

Goodbye for now, ma'am. She pictured herself making her curtsey and Morgan le Fay smiling on her. She pictured taking Peter's rough lean hand, shaking it, looking straight into those eyes of his without fear or shame.

She'd done well. They'd all done well. Together.

Between them, Peter and the Fay helped her to the door, opened it, and ushered her through. Almost before the door had closed behind her, they were talking again.

"Of course the next time she comes down, we'll have things more comfortable around here. The ale's all gone and there's nothing to sit on except that red contraption over there. And then there's the smell of your horse . . ."

Smiling contentedly, Meg made for the stairs.

— — —

Meg awoke to a loud buzzing in her ears and light flashing in her eyes. For one confused moment, she thought herself back in the Dark World.

But then the buzzing stopped abruptly and she heard a distant voice.

Father's. Downstairs.

She sighed, uncurled, and opened her eyes.

The sun was shining straight into them.

Sue must have drawn back her curtains and pulled up her blind. She always did that when she wanted Meg to wake up.

There was a rush of feet on the stairs and Sue burst in.

"Meg! Meg, wake up! It's Mrs. Thorpe!"

Meg leapt out of bed and collided with Father. He caught her arm. "Meg, there's a Mrs. Thorpe on the phone. She says you know her son, Gavin Owen. Apparently he's in the hospital and demanding to see you. She wants to know how soon you can get there."

Meg was already out of the door and halfway down the stairs, with Sue at her heels, before Father added, "It's strange that I've never met him."

Meg called back over her shoulder. "I know, but you will, very soon."

She picked up the phone.

"Hello? Hello, Mrs. Thorpe? Yes. I'm Meg Wilson. Yes. I'd like that very much. My sister too." Meg half turned to Sue, who was standing squeezed up against her, trying to listen in. She grinned, gave her the thumbs up sign. "Pardon? Well, yes, it does seem strange. Yes, we surely do have a lot of talking to do. Yes, oh, yes. We surely can be there by lunchtime. Please tell Gavin we can hardly wait!"

She listened, smiling, making happy faces at Sue all the while.

She put down the phone, grabbed Sue, and waltzed her around and around, then up the stairs.

"What is it, Meg?" Sue cried, laughing, and tripping on the stairs. "Was it—did it go right? Did you do it?"

"Did *we* do it, you mean. We sure did!" Meg tightened her grip and jumped Sue up and down.

She turned to Father, standing puzzled in his study doorway.

"Father, may Sue and I go into the city today? You come, too, if you like. Our brand-new cousin's just invited us to lunch!"